# The Brothers Grimm's
## Fairy Tales

Paper Mill Press Illustrated Classics
is an imprint of Book Depot Inc.
67 Front Street North, Thorold, L2V 1X3 Canada
Printed in China
www.bookdepot.com
Selection, design, arrangement, typesetting, and image reproduction all copyright.
©2022 North Parade Publishing
All rights reserved

ISBN: 978-1-77402-222-1

25 24 23 22 • 5 4 3 2 1

# The Brothers Grimm's

## Fairy Tales

by

# Jacob & Wilhelm Grimm

with illustrations by

Arthur Rackham

# Contents

# Color Illustrations

# Introduction

For two hundred years, the stories brought together by the Brothers Grimm have enchanted, frightened, and amused both children and adults alike, for we are never too old to feel the power of their fascination. "Cinderella," "Hansel and Gretel," "Little Red Riding Hood," "Rumpelstiltskin"—these are all household names, and are an essential part of our childhood experience, not only as a source of interest and amusement, but also because of the homely wisdom that these tales impart. All we need to hear are the words "Once upon a time" and we are transported into a realm of fairies and princesses, witches and goblins, castles and dragons.

But how well do we know these stories? We are familiar and comfortable with Disney's rose-tinted view of the world and penchant for "happily ever after" endings, but did Cinderella really go to the ball in a pumpkin carriage with the help of a fairy godmother, and how did the evil queen really get her comeuppance in "Snow White"?

It is worthwhile to go back to the original stories, many of which are rather darker than the film versions that we know and love. Indeed, some of them were darker still on original publication—so much so that they were not all deemed suitable for children, and changes were made to make them more palatable: evil mothers became wicked stepmothers, no longer does Rapunzel become pregnant from the prince's visits and betray her indiscretion by her bulging waistline, and some stories were cut altogether!

Titles have changed too: we are more familiar with "Sleeping Beauty" than with "Briar Rose," or with "Cinderella" than "Ashenputtel," and here we have chosen to use the more popular names. This version is based, with a few updates, on the first English translation by Edgar Taylor from the 1820s, modified at the start of the following century by Marian Edwardes. We have included some of the most popular stories, and some less well known, all illustrated with original artwork by the acclaimed Victorian illustrator Sir Arthur Rackham.

Let the magic begin . . .

# The Golden Bird.

A certain king had a beautiful garden, and in the garden stood a tree which bore golden apples. These apples were always counted, and about the time when they began to grow ripe it was found that every night one of them was gone. The king became very angry at this, and ordered the gardener to keep watch all night under the tree. The gardener set his eldest son to watch; but at about twelve o'clock he fell asleep, and in the morning another of the apples was missing. Then the second son was ordered to watch; and at midnight he too fell asleep, and in the morning another apple was gone. Then the third son offered to keep watch; but the gardener at first would not let him, for fear some harm should come to him: however, at last he consented, and the young man laid himself under the tree to watch. As the clock struck twelve he heard a rustling noise in the air, and a bird came flying that was of pure gold; and as it was snapping at one of the apples with its beak, the gardener's son jumped up and shot an arrow at it. But the arrow did the bird no harm; only it dropped a golden feather from its tail, and then flew away. The golden feather was brought to the king in the morning, and all the council was called together. Everyone agreed that it was worth more than all the wealth of the kingdom: but the king said, "One feather is of no use to me, I must have the whole bird."

Then the gardener's eldest son set out and thought to find the golden bird very easily; and when he had gone but a little way, he came to a wood, and by the side of the wood he saw a fox sitting; so he took his bow and made ready to shoot at it.

Then the fox said, "Do not shoot me, for I will give you good counsel; I know what your business is, and that you want to find the golden bird. You will reach a village in the evening; and when you get there, you will see two inns opposite to each other, one of which is very pleasant and beautiful to look at: go not in there, but rest for the night in the other, though it may appear to you to be very poor and mean."

But the son thought to himself, "What can such a beast as this know about the matter?" So he shot his arrow at the fox; but he missed it, and it set up its tail above its back and ran into the wood.

Then he went his way, and in the evening came to the village where the two inns were; and in one of these were people singing, and dancing, and feasting; but the other looked very dirty, and poor. "I should be very silly," said he, "if I went to that shabby house, and left this charming place"; so he went into the smart house, and ate and drank at his ease, and forgot the bird, and his country too.

Time passed on and as the eldest son did not come back, and no tidings were heard of him, the second son set out, and the same thing happened to him. He met the fox, who gave him the good advice: but when he came to the two inns, his elder brother was standing at the window where the merrymaking was, and called to him to come in; and he could not withstand the temptation, but went in, and forgot the golden bird and his country in the same manner.

Time passed on again, and the youngest son too wished to set out into the wide world to seek for the golden bird; but his father would not listen to his entreaties for a long while, for he was very fond of his son, and was afraid that some ill luck might happen to him also, and prevent his coming back. However, at last it was agreed he should go, for he would not rest at home; and as he came to the wood, he met the fox, and heard the same good counsel. But he was thankful to the fox, and did not attempt his life as his brothers had done; so the fox said, "Sit upon my tail, and you will travel faster." So he sat down, and the fox began to run, and away they went over hill and dale so quick that their hair whistled in the wind.

When they came to the village, the son followed the fox's counsel, and without looking about him went to the shabby inn and rested there all night at his ease. In the morning came the fox again and met him as he was beginning his journey, and said, "Go straight forward till you come to a castle, before which lie a whole troop of soldiers fast asleep and snoring: take no notice of them, but go into the castle and pass on and on till you come to a room, where the golden bird sits in a wooden cage; close by it stands a beautiful golden cage; but do not try to take the bird out of the shabby cage and put it into the handsome one, otherwise you will repent it." Then the fox stretched out his tail again, and the young man sat himself down, and away they went over hill and dale till their hair whistled in the wind.

Before the castle gate all was as the fox had said: so the son went in and found the chamber where the golden bird hung in a wooden cage, and below stood the golden cage, and the three golden apples that had been lost were lying close by it. Then thought he to himself, "It will be a very droll thing to bring away such a fine bird in this shabby cage"; so he opened the door and took hold of it and put it into the golden cage. But the bird set up such a loud scream that all the soldiers awoke, and they took him prisoner and carried him before the king. The next morning the court sat to judge him; and when all was heard,

*Away they went over hill and dale so quick that their hair whistled in the wind.*

it sentenced him to die, unless he should bring the king the golden horse which could run as swiftly as the wind; and if he did this, he was to have the golden bird given him for his own.

So he set out once more on his journey, sighing, and in great despair, when on a sudden his friend the fox met him, and said, "You see now what has happened on account of your not listening to my counsel. I will still, however, tell you how to find the golden horse, if you will do as I bid you. You must go straight on till you come to the castle where the horse stands in his stall: by his side will lie the groom fast asleep and snoring: take away the horse quietly, but be sure to put the old leathern saddle upon him, and not the golden one that is close by it." Then the son sat down on the fox's tail, and away they went over hill and dale till their hair whistled in the wind.

All went right, and the groom lay snoring with his hand upon the golden saddle. But when the son looked at the horse, he thought it a great pity to put the leathern saddle upon it. "I will give him the good one," said he; "I am sure he deserves it." As he took up the golden saddle the groom awoke and cried out so loud that all the guards ran in and took him prisoner, and in the morning he was again brought before the court to be judged, and was sentenced to die. But it was agreed, that, if he could bring thither the beautiful princess, he should live, and have the bird and the horse given him for his own.

Then he went his way very sorrowful; but the old fox came and said, "Why did you not listen to me? If you had, you would have carried away both the bird and the horse; yet will I once more give you counsel. Go straight on, and in the evening you will arrive at a castle. At twelve o'clock at night the princess goes to the bathing-house: go up to her and give her a kiss, and she will let you lead her away; but take care you do not suffer her to go and take leave of her father and mother." Then the fox stretched out his tail, and so away they went over hill and dale till their hair whistled again.

As they came to the castle, all was as the fox had said, and at twelve o'clock the young man met the princess going to the bath and gave her the kiss, and she agreed to run away with him, but begged with many tears that he would let her take leave of her father. At first he refused, but she wept still more and more, and fell at his feet, till at last he consented; but the moment she came to her father's house the guards awoke and he was taken prisoner again.

Then he was brought before the king, and the king said, "You shall never have my daughter unless in eight days you dig away the hill that stops the view from my window."

Now this hill was so big that the whole world could not take it away: and when he had worked for seven days, and had done very little, the fox came and said, "Lie down and go to sleep; I will work for you." And in the morning he awoke and the hill was gone; so he went merrily to the king, and told him that now that it was removed he must give him the princess.

Then the king was obliged to keep his word, and away went the young man and the princess; and the fox came and said to him, "We will have all three, the princess, the horse, and the bird."

"Ah!" said the young man, "that would be a great thing, but how can you contrive it?"

"If you will only listen," said the fox, "it can be done. When you come to the king, and he asks for the beautiful princess, you must say, 'Here she is!' Then he will be very joyful; and you will mount the golden horse that they are to give you, and put out your hand to take leave of them; but shake hands with the princess last. Then lift her quickly onto the horse behind you; clap your spurs to his side, and gallop away as fast as you can."

All went just so. Then the fox said, "When you come to the castle where the bird is, I will stay with the princess at the door, and you will ride in and speak to the king; and when he sees that it is the right horse, he will bring out the bird; but you must sit still, and say that you want to look at it, to see whether it is the true golden bird; and when

you get it into your hand, ride away."

This, too, happened as the fox said; the young man carried off the bird, the princess mounted again, and they rode on to a great wood. Then the fox came, and said, "Pray kill me, and cut off my head and my feet." But the young man refused to do it: so the fox said, "I will at any rate give you good counsel: beware of two things; ransom no one from the gallows, and sit down by the side of no river." Then away he went.

"Well," thought the young man, "it is no hard matter to keep that advice."

He rode on with the princess, till at last he came to the village where he had left his two brothers. And there he heard a great noise and uproar; and when he asked what was the matter, the people said, "Two men are going to be hanged."

As he came nearer, he saw that the two men were his brothers, who had turned robbers; so he said, "Cannot they in any way be saved?"

But the people said no, not unless he would bestow all his money upon the rascals and buy their liberty. Then he did not stay to think about the matter, but paid what was asked, and his brothers were given up, and went on with him towards their home.

And as they came to the wood where the fox first met them, it was so cool and pleasant that the two brothers said, "Let us sit down by the side of the river, and rest a while, to eat and drink."

So he said, "Yes," and forgot the fox's counsel, and sat down on the side of the river; and while he suspected nothing, they came behind, and threw him down the bank, and took the princess, the horse, and the bird, and went home to the king their master, and said, "All this have we won by our labor." Then there was great rejoicing made; but the horse would not eat, the bird would not sing, and the princess wept.

The youngest son fell to the bottom of the river's bed: luckily it was nearly dry, but his bones were almost broken, and the bank was so steep that he could find no way to get out. Then the old fox came once more, and scolded him for not following his advice; otherwise no evil would have befallen him. "Yet," said he, "I cannot leave you here, so lay hold of my tail and hold fast." Then he pulled him out of the river, and said to him, as he got upon the bank, "Your brothers have set watch to kill you, if they find you in the kingdom."

So he dressed himself as a poor man, and came secretly to the king's court, and was scarcely within the doors when the horse began to eat, and the bird to sing, and the princess left off weeping. Then he went to the king, and told him all his brothers' roguery; and they were seized and punished, and he had the princess given to him again; and after the king's death he was heir to his kingdom.

A long while after, he went to walk one day in the wood, and the old fox met him, and besought him with tears in his eyes to kill him, and cut off his head and feet. And at last he did so, and in a moment the fox was changed into a man, and turned out to be the brother of the princess, who had been lost a very great many years.

# HANS IN LUCK

Some men are born to good luck: all they do or try to do comes right, all that falls to them is so much gain, all their geese are swans, all their cards are trumps—toss them which way you will, they will always, like poor puss, alight upon their legs, and only move on so much the faster. The world may very likely not always think of them as they think of themselves, but what care they for the world? What can it know about the matter?

One of these lucky beings was neighbor Hans. Seven long years he had worked hard for his master. At last he said, "Master, my time is up; I must go home and see my poor mother once more; so pray pay me my wages and let me go."

And the master said, "You have been a faithful and good servant, Hans, so your pay shall be handsome." Then he gave him a lump of silver as big as his head.

Hans took out his pocket-handkerchief, put the piece of silver into it, threw it over his shoulder, and set off on his road homewards. As he went lazily on, dragging one foot after another, a man came in sight, trotting gaily along on a capital horse.

"Ah!" said Hans aloud, "what a fine thing it is to ride on horseback! There he sits as easy and happy as if he was at home, in the chair by his fireside; he trips against no stones, saves shoe-leather and gets where he's going he hardly knows how."

Hans did not speak softly so the horseman heard it all. "Well, friend, why do you go on foot then?" he asked.

"Ah!" said Hans, "I have this load to carry: to be sure it is silver, but it is so heavy that I can't hold up my head, and I can tell you it hurts my shoulder sadly."

"What do you say of making an exchange?" said the horseman. "I will give you my horse, and you shall give me the silver; which will save you a great deal of trouble in carrying such a heavy load about with you."

"With all my heart," said Hans: "but as you are so kind to me, I must tell you one thing—you will have a weary task to draw that silver about with you."

Undeterred, the horseman got off, took the silver, helped Hans up, gave him the bridle into one hand and the whip into the other, and said, "When you want to go very fast, smack your lips loudly together, and cry 'Jip!'"

Hans was delighted as he sat on the horse, drew himself up, squared his elbows, turned out his toes, cracked his whip, and rode merrily off, one minute whistling a merry tune, and another singing,

> *"No care and no sorrow,*
> *A fig for the morrow!*
> *We'll laugh and be merry,*
> *Sing neigh down derry!"*

After a time he thought he should like to go a little faster, so he smacked his lips and cried "Jip!" Away went the horse at full gallop; and before Hans knew what he was about, he was thrown off, and lay on his back by the roadside. His horse would have run off, if a shepherd who was coming by, driving a cow, had not stopped it. Hans soon came to himself, and got upon his legs again, sadly vexed, and said to the shepherd, "This riding is no joke for a man who has the luck to get upon a beast like this that stumbles and flings him off as if it would break his neck. However, I'm off now once and for all! I like your cow now a great deal better than this smart beast that played me this trick, and has spoiled my best coat, as you see, in this puddle; which, by the by, smells not very like a nosegay. One can walk along at one's leisure behind that cow—keep good company, and have milk, butter, and cheese every day into the bargain. What would I give to have such a prize!"

"Well," said the shepherd, "if you are so fond of her, I will change my cow for your horse; I like to do good to my neighbors, even though I lose by it myself."

"Done!" said Hans, merrily. "What a noble heart that good man has!" thought he. Then the shepherd jumped upon the horse, wished Hans and the cow good morning, and away he rode.

Hans brushed his coat, wiped his face and hands, rested a while, and then drove off his cow quietly, and thought his bargain a very lucky one. "If I have only a piece of bread (and I certainly shall always be able to get that), I can, whenever I like, eat my butter and cheese with it; and when I am thirsty I can milk my cow and drink the milk: who could wish for more?" When he came to an inn, he halted, ate up all his bread, and gave away his last penny for a glass of beer. When he had rested himself he set off again, driving his cow towards his mother's village. But the heat grew greater as soon as noon came on, till at last, as he found himself on a wide heath that would take him more than an hour to cross, he began to be so hot and parched that his tongue cleaved to the roof of his mouth. "I can find a cure for this," thought he; "now I will milk my cow and quench my thirst": so he tied her to the stump of a tree, and held his leathern cap to milk into; but not a drop was to be had. Who would have thought that this cow, which was to bring him milk and butter and cheese, was all the time utterly dry? Hans had not even considered the possibility.

While he was trying his luck in milking, and managing the matter very clumsily, the uneasy beast began to think him very troublesome; and at last she gave him such a kick on the head that she knocked him

down; and there he lay a long while senseless. Luckily a butcher soon
came by, pushing a pig in a wheelbarrow.

"What is the matter with you, my man?" said the butcher, as he
helped him up.

Hans told him what had happened, how he was dry, and wanted
to milk his cow, but found the cow was dry too. Then the butcher

gave him a flask of ale, saying, "There, drink and refresh yourself; your cow will give you no milk: don't you see she is an old beast, good for nothing but the slaughterhouse?"

"Alas, alas!" said Hans, "who would have thought it? What a shame to take my horse, and give me only a dry cow! If I kill her, what will she be good for? I hate cow-beef; it is not tender enough for me. If she were a pig now—like that fat gentleman you are wheeling along at his ease— one could do something with her; she would at any rate make sausages."

"Well," said the butcher, "I don't like to say no, when one is asked to do a kind, neighborly thing. To please you I will change, and give you my fine fat pig for the cow."

"Heaven reward you for your kindness and self-denial!" said Hans, as he gave the butcher the cow; and taking the pig off the wheelbarrow, drove it away, holding it by the string that was tied to its leg.

So on he jogged, and all seemed now to go right with him: he had met with some misfortunes, to be sure; but he was now well repaid for all. How could it be otherwise with such a traveling companion as he had at last got?

The next man he met was a countryman carrying a fine white goose. The countryman stopped to ask him the time; this led to further chat; and Hans told him all his luck, how he had had so many good bargains, and how all the world had seemed to be smiling with him. The countryman then began to tell his tale, and said he was going to take the goose to a christening. "Feel," said he, "how heavy it is, and yet it is only eight weeks old. Whoever roasts and eats it will find plenty of fat upon it, it has lived so well!"

"You're right," said Hans, as he weighed it in his hands; "but if you talk of fat, my pig is no trifle."

Meantime the countryman began to look grave, and shook his head. "Hark ye," said he, "my worthy friend, you seem a good sort of fellow, so I can't help doing you a kind turn. Your pig may get you into a scrape. In the village I just came from, the squire has had a pig stolen out of his sty.

I was dreadfully afraid when I saw you that you had got the squire's pig. If you have, and they catch you, it will be a bad job for you. The least they will do will be to throw you into the horse-pond. Can you swim?"

Poor Hans was sadly frightened. "Good man," cried he, "pray get me out of this scrape. I know nothing of where the pig was either bred or born; but he may have been the squire's for aught I can tell: you know this country better than I do, take my pig and give me the goose."

"I ought to have something into the bargain," said the countryman; "give a fat goose for a pig, indeed! 'Tis not everyone would do so much for you as that. However, I will not be hard upon you, as you are in trouble."

Then he took the string in his hand, and drove off the pig by a side path, while Hans went on the way homewards free from care. "After all," thought he, "that chap is pretty well taken in. I don't care whose pig it is, but wherever it came from, in this it has been a very good friend to me. I have much the best of the bargain. First there will be a capital roast; then the fat will find me in goose-grease for six months; and then there are all the beautiful white feathers. I will put them into my pillow, and then I am sure I shall sleep soundly without rocking. How happy my mother will be! Talk of a pig, indeed! Give me a fine fat goose."

As he came to the next village, he saw a scissor-grinder with his wheel, working and singing,

*"O'er hill and o'er dale*
*So happy I roam,*
*Work light and live well,*
*All the world is my home;*
*Then who so blithe, so merry as I?"*

Hans stood looking on for a while, and at last said, "You must be well off, master grinder! You seem so happy at your work."

"Yes," said the other, "mine is a golden trade; a good grinder never puts his hand into his pocket without finding money in it—but where did you get that beautiful goose?"

"I did not buy it, I gave a pig for it."

"And where did you get the pig?"

"I gave a cow for it."

"And the cow?"

"I gave a horse for it."

"And the horse?"

"I gave a lump of silver as big as my head for it."

"And the silver?"

"Oh! I worked hard for that seven long years."

"You have thrived well in the world hitherto," said the grinder, "now if you could find money in your pocket whenever you put your hand in it, your fortune would be made."

"Very true, but how is that to be managed?"

"How? Why, you must turn grinder like myself," said the other; "you only want a grindstone; the rest will come of itself. Here is one that is but little the worse for wear. I would not ask more than the value of your goose for it—will you buy?"

"How can you ask?" said Hans. "I should be the happiest man in the world, if I could have money whenever I put my hand in my pocket: what could I want more? There's the goose."

"Now," said the grinder, as he gave him a common rough stone that lay by his side, "this is a most capital stone; do but work it well enough, and you can make an old nail cut with it."

Hans took the stone, and went his way with a light heart; his eyes sparkled for joy, and he said to himself, "Surely I must have been born in a lucky hour; everything I could want or wish for comes of itself. People are so kind; they seem really to think I do them a favor in letting them make me rich, and giving me good bargains."

Meantime he began to be tired, and hungry too, for he had given away his last penny in his joy at getting the cow.

At last he could go no farther, for the stone tired him sadly, and he dragged himself to the side of a river, that he might take a drink of water, and rest a while. He laid the stone carefully by his side on the bank: but, as he stooped down to drink, he forgot it, pushed it a little, and down it rolled, plump into the stream.

For a while he watched it sinking in the deep clear water—then sprang up and danced for joy, and again fell upon his knees and thanked heaven, with tears in his eyes, for its kindness in taking away his only plague, the ugly heavy stone.

"How happy am I!" cried he; "nobody was ever so lucky as I." Then up he got with a light heart, free from all his troubles, and walked on till he reached his mother's house, and told her how very easy the road to good luck was.

# THE TRAVELING MUSICIANS

A n honest farmer had once an ass that had been a faithful servant to him a great many years, but was now growing old and every day more and more unfit for work. His master therefore was tired of keeping him and began to think of putting an end to him; but the ass, who saw that some mischief was in the wind, took himself slyly off, and began his journey towards the great city, "For there," thought he, "I may turn musician."

After he had traveled a little way, he spied a dog lying by the roadside and panting as if he were tired. "What makes you pant so, my friend?" said the ass.

"Alas!" said the dog, "my master was going to knock me on the head, because I am old and weak, and can no longer make myself useful to him in hunting; so I ran away; but what can I do to earn my livelihood?"

"Hark ye!" said the ass, "I am going to the great city to turn musician: suppose you come with me, and see what you can do in the same way?" The dog said he was willing, and they jogged on together.

They had not gone far before they saw a cat sitting in the middle of the road and making a most rueful face.

"Pray, my good lady," said the ass, "what's the matter with you? You look quite out of spirits!"

"Ah, me!" said the cat, "how can one be in good spirits when one's life is in danger? Because I am beginning to grow old, and had rather lie at my ease by the fire than run about the house after the mice, my mistress laid hold of me, and was going to drown me; and though I

have been lucky enough to get away from her, I do not know what I am to live upon."

"Oh," said the ass, "by all means come with us to the great city; you are a good night singer, and may make your fortune as a musician." The cat was pleased with the thought, and joined the party.

Soon afterwards, as they were passing by a farmyard, they saw a cock perched upon a gate, and screaming out with all his might and main. "Bravo!" said the ass; "upon my word, you make a famous noise; pray what is all this about?"

"Why," said the cock, "I was just now saying that we should have fine weather for our washing-day, and yet my mistress and the cook don't thank me for my pains, but threaten to cut off my head tomorrow, and make broth of me for the guests that are coming on Sunday!"

"Heaven forbid!" said the ass, "come with us, Master Chanticleer; it will be better, at any rate, than staying here to have your head cut off! Besides, who knows? If we care to sing in tune, we may get up some kind of a concert; so come along with us."

"With all my heart," said the cock; so they all four went on jollily together.

They could not, however, reach the great city the first day; so when night came on, they went into a wood to sleep. The ass and the dog laid themselves down under a great tree, and the cat climbed up into the branches; while the cock, thinking that the higher he sat the safer he should be, flew up to the very top of the tree, and then, according to his custom, before he went to sleep, looked out on all sides of him to see that everything was well. In doing this, he saw afar off something bright and shining, and calling to his companions said, "There must be a house no great way off, for I see a light."

"If that be the case," said the ass, "we had better change our quarters, for our lodging is not the best in the world!"

"Besides," added the dog, "I should not be the worse for a bone or two, or a bit of meat." So they walked off together towards the spot where Chanticleer had seen the light, and as they drew near it became larger and brighter, till they at last came close to a house in which a gang of robbers lived.

The ass, being the tallest of the company, marched up to the window and peeped in. "Well, donkey," said Chanticleer, "what do you see?"

"What do I see?" replied the ass. "Why, I see a table spread with all kinds of good things, and robbers sitting round it making merry."

"That would be a noble lodging for us," said the cock. "Yes," said the ass, "if we could only get in"; so they consulted together how they should contrive to get the robbers out; and at last they hit upon a plan. The ass placed himself upright on his hind legs, with his forefeet resting against the window; the dog got upon his back; the cat scrambled up to the dog's shoulders; and the cock flew up and sat upon the cat's head. When all was ready a signal was given, and they began their music. The ass brayed, the dog barked, the cat mewed, and the cock screamed; and then they all broke through the window at once, and came tumbling into the room, among the broken glass, with a most hideous clatter! The robbers, who had been not a little frightened by the opening concert, had now no doubt that some frightful hobgoblin had broken in upon them, and scampered away as fast as they could.

The coast once clear, our travelers soon sat down and dispatched what the robbers had left, with as much eagerness as if they had not expected to eat again for a month. As soon as they had satisfied themselves, they put out the lights, and each once more sought out a resting-place to his own liking. The donkey laid himself down upon a heap of straw in the yard, the dog stretched himself upon a mat behind the door, the cat rolled herself up on the hearth before the warm ashes, and the cock perched upon a beam on the top of the house; and, as they were all rather tired with their journey, they soon fell asleep.

But about midnight, when the robbers saw from afar that the lights were out and that all seemed quiet, they began to think that they had been in too great a hurry to run away; and one of them, who was bolder than the rest, went to see what was going on. Finding everything still, he marched into the kitchen, and groped about till he found a match in order to light a candle; and then, espying the glittering fiery eyes of the cat, he mistook them for live coals, and held the match to them to light it. But the cat, not understanding this joke, sprang at his face, and spat, and scratched at him. This frightened him dreadfully, and away he ran to the back door; but there the dog jumped up and bit him in the leg; and as he was crossing over the yard the ass kicked him; and the cock, who had been awakened by the noise, crowed with all his might. At this the robber ran back as fast as he could to his comrades, and told the captain how a horrid witch had got into the house, and had spat at him and scratched his face with her long bony fingers; how a man with a knife in his hand had hidden himself behind the door, and stabbed him in the leg; how a black monster stood in the yard and struck him with a club, and how the devil had sat upon the top of the house and cried out, "Throw the rascal up here!" After this the robbers never dared to go back to the house; but the musicians were so pleased with their quarters that they took up their abode there; and there they are, I dare say, at this very day.

*She crept about the country like a cat . . .*

# JORINDA AND JORINDEL

T here was once an old castle that stood in the middle of a deep gloomy wood, and in the castle lived an old fairy. Now this fairy could take any shape she pleased. All the day long she flew about in the form of an owl, or crept about the country like a cat; but at night she always became an old woman again.

*. . . or flew about in the form of an owl.*

When any young man came within a hundred paces of her castle, he became quite fixed, and could not move a step till she came and set him free; which she would not do till he had given her his word never to come there again. But when any pretty maiden came within that space she was changed into a bird, and the fairy put her into a cage, and hung her up in a chamber in the castle. There were seven hundred of these cages hanging in the castle, and all with beautiful birds in them.

Now there was once a maiden whose name was Jorinda. She was prettier than all the pretty girls that ever were seen before, and a shepherd lad, whose name was Jorindel, was very fond of her, and they were soon to be married.

One day they went to walk in the wood, that they might be alone; and Jorindel said, "We must take care that we don't go too near to the fairy's castle." It was a beautiful evening; the last rays of the setting sun shone bright through the long stems of the trees upon the green underwood beneath, and the turtledoves sang from the tall birches.

Jorinda sat down to gaze upon the sun; Jorindel sat by her side and both felt sad, they knew not why; but it seemed as if they were to be parted from one another forever. They had wandered a long way; and when they looked to see which way they should go home, they found themselves at a loss to know what path to take.

The sun was setting fast, and already half of its circle had sunk behind the hill. Jorindel suddenly looked behind him, and saw through the bushes that they had, without knowing it, sat down close under the old walls of the castle. Then he shrank for fear, turned pale, and trembled. Jorinda was just singing,

> *"The ring-dove sang from the willow spray,*
> *Well-a-day! Well-a-day!*
> *He mourn'd for the fate of his darling mate,*
> *Well-a-day!"*

when her song stopped suddenly. Jorindel turned to see the reason, and beheld his Jorinda changed into a nightingale, so that her song ended with a mournful "jug, jug." An owl with fiery eyes flew three times round them, and three times screamed: "Tu whu! Tu whu! Tu whu!"

Jorindel could not move; he stood fixed as a stone, and could neither weep, nor speak, nor stir hand or foot. And now the sun went quite down; the gloomy night came; the owl flew into a bush; and a moment after the old fairy came forth pale and meager, with staring eyes, and a nose and chin that almost met one another.

She mumbled something to herself, seized the nightingale, and went away with it in her hand. Poor Jorindel saw the nightingale was gone—but what could he do? He could not speak; he could not move from the spot where he stood. At last the fairy came back and sang with a hoarse voice:

> "Till the prisoner is fast,
> And her doom is cast,
> There stay! Oh, stay!
> When the charm is around her,
> And the spell has bound her,
> Hie away! away!"

Suddenly Jorindel found himself free. Then he fell on his knees before the fairy, and prayed her to give him back his dear Jorinda; but she laughed at him, and said he should never see her again; then she went her way.

He prayed, he wept, he sorrowed, but all in vain. "Alas!" he said, "what will become of me?" He could not go back to his own home, so he went to a strange village, and employed himself in keeping sheep. Many a time did he walk round and round as near to the hated castle as he dared go, but all in vain; he neither heard nor saw anything of Jorinda.

At last he dreamt one night that he found a beautiful purple flower, and that in the middle of it lay a costly pearl; and he dreamt that he plucked the flower, and went with it in his hand into the castle, and that everything he touched with it was disenchanted, and that there he found his Jorinda again.

In the morning when he awoke, he began to search over hill and dale for this pretty flower. For eight long days he sought for it in vain, but on the ninth day, early in the morning, he found the beautiful purple flower; and in the middle of it was a large dewdrop, as big as a costly pearl. Then he plucked the flower, and set out and traveled day and night till he came again to the castle.

He walked nearer than a hundred paces to it, and yet he did not become fixed as before, but found that he could go quite close up to the door. Jorindel was very glad indeed to see this. Then he touched the door with the flower, and it sprang open; so that he went in through the court, and listened when he heard so many birds singing. At last he came to the chamber where the fairy sat, with the seven hundred birds singing in the seven hundred cages. When she saw Jorindel she was very angry, and screamed with rage; but she could not come within two yards of him, for the flower he held in his hand was his safeguard. He looked around at the birds, but alas! there were many, many nightingales, and he was at a loss to find out which was his Jorinda. While he was thinking what to do, he saw the fairy had taken down one of the cages, and was making off with it through the door. He ran—or flew—after her, touched the cage with the flower, and Jorinda stood before him, and threw her arms round his neck looking as beautiful as ever, as beautiful as when they walked together in the wood.

Then he touched all the other birds with the flower, so that they all took their old forms again; and he took Jorinda home, where they were married, and lived happily together many years: and so did a good many other lads, whose maidens had been forced to sing in the old fairy's cages by themselves much longer than they liked.

*Just as Little Red Riding Hood entered the wood, a wolf met her.*

# LITTLE RED RIDING HOOD

Once upon a time there was a dear little girl who was loved by everyone who looked at her, but most of all by her grandmother, and there was nothing that she would not have given to the child. Once she gave her a little cap of red velvet, which suited her so well that she would never wear anything else; so she was always called "Little Red Riding Hood."

One day her mother said to her: "Come, Little Red Riding Hood, here is a piece of cake and a bottle of wine; take them to your grandmother, for she is ill and weak and they will do her good. Set out before it gets hot, and when you are going, walk nicely and quietly and do not run off the path, or you may fall and break the bottle, and then your grandmother will get nothing; and when you go into her room, don't forget to say, 'Good morning,' and don't peep into every corner before you do it."

"I will take great care," said Little Red Riding Hood to her mother, and gave her hand on it.

The grandmother lived out in the wood, half a league from the village, and just as Little Red Riding Hood entered the wood, a wolf met her. Little Red Riding Hood did not know what a wicked creature he was, and was not at all afraid of him.

"Good day, Little Red Riding Hood," said he.

"Thank you kindly, wolf."

"Whither away so early, Little Red Riding Hood?"

"To my grandmother's."

"What have you got in your apron?"

"Cake and wine; yesterday was baking day, so poor sick grandmother is to have something good, to make her stronger."

"Where does your grandmother live, Little Red Riding Hood?"

"A good quarter of a league farther on in the wood; her house stands under the three large oak trees, the nut trees are just below; you surely must know it," replied Little Red Riding Hood.

The wolf thought to himself: "What a tender young creature! What a nice plump mouthful—she will be better to eat than the old woman. I must act craftily, so as to catch both." So he walked for a short time by the side of Little Red Riding Hood, and then he said: "Little Red Riding Hood, how pretty the flowers are about here—why do you not look round? I believe, too, that you do not hear how sweetly the little birds are singing; you walk gravely along as if you were going to school, while everything else out here in the wood is merry."

Little Red Riding Hood raised her eyes, and when she saw the sunbeams dancing here and there through the trees, and pretty flowers growing everywhere, she thought: "Suppose I take grandmother a fresh nosegay; that would please her too. It is so early in the day that I shall still get there in good time"; and so she ran from the path into the wood to look for flowers. And whenever she had picked one, she fancied that she saw a still prettier one farther on, and ran after it, and so got deeper and deeper into the wood.

Meanwhile the wolf ran straight to the grandmother's house and knocked at the door.

"Who is there?"

"Little Red Riding Hood," replied the wolf. "I have brought cake and wine; open the door."

"Lift the latch," called out the grandmother. "I am too weak, and cannot get up."

The wolf lifted the latch, the door sprang open, and without saying a word he went straight to the grandmother's bed and devoured her.

Then he put on her clothes, dressed himself in her cap, laid himself in bed, and drew the curtains.

Little Red Riding Hood, however, had been running about picking flowers, and when she had gathered so many that she could carry no more, she remembered her grandmother, and set out on the way to her.

She was surprised to find the cottage door standing open, and when she went into the room she had such a strange feeling that she said to herself: "Oh dear! How uneasy I feel today, and at other times I like being with grandmother so much." She called out: "Good morning," but received no answer; so she went to the bed and drew back the curtains. There lay her grandmother wearing her cap all askew and looking very strange.

"Oh, grandmother," she said, "what big ears you have!"

"The better to hear you with, my child," was the reply.

"But, grandmother, what big eyes you have!" she said.

"The better to see you with, my dear."

"But, grandmother, what large hands you have!"

"The better to hug you with."

"Oh but, grandmother, what a terrible big mouth you have!"

"The better to eat you with!"

And scarcely had the wolf said this, than with one bound he was out of bed and had swallowed up Little Red Riding Hood.

When the wolf had appeased his appetite, he lay down again in the bed, fell asleep, and began to snore very loud. The huntsman was just passing the house, and thought to himself: "How the old woman is snoring! I must just see if she wants anything." So he went into the room, and when he came to the bed, he saw that the wolf was lying in it. "Do I find you here, you old sinner!" said he. "I have long sought you!" Then just as he was going to fire at him, it occurred to him that the wolf might have devoured the grandmother, and that she might still be saved, so he did not fire, but took a pair of scissors, and began to cut open the stomach of the sleeping wolf. When he had made two

*"Oh, grandmother," she said, "what big ears you have!"*

snips, he saw the little red riding hood shining, and then he made two snips more, and the little girl sprang out, crying: "Ah, how frightened I have been! How dark it was inside the wolf!" After that the aged grandmother came out alive also, but scarcely able to breathe. Little Red Riding Hood, however, quickly fetched great stones with which they filled the wolf's belly, and when he awoke, he wanted to run away, but the stones were so heavy that he collapsed at once, and fell dead.

Then all three were delighted. The huntsman drew off the wolf's skin and went home with it; the grandmother ate the cake and drank the wine which Little Red Riding Hood had brought and was greatly revived; and Little Red Riding Hood thought to herself: "As long as I live, I will never by myself leave the path, to run into the wood, when my mother has forbidden me to do so."

And so it happened that when Little Red Riding Hood was again taking cakes to the old grandmother, and another wolf spoke to her, and tried to entice her from the path, Little Red Riding Hood was on her guard, and went straight forward on her way, and told her grandmother that she had met the wolf, and that he had said "good morning" to her, but with such a wicked look in his eyes that if they had not been on the public road she was certain he would have eaten her up.

"Well," said the grandmother, "we will shut the door, that he may not come in."

Soon afterwards the wolf knocked, and cried: "Open the door, grandmother, I am Little Red Riding Hood, and am bringing you some cakes."

But they did not speak, or open the door, so the gray-beard crept twice or thrice round the house, and at last jumped on the roof, intending to wait until Little Red Riding Hood went home in the evening, and then to steal after her and devour her in the darkness.

But the grandmother saw what was in his thoughts. In front of the house was a great stone trough, so she said to the child: "Take the pail, Little Red Riding Hood; I made some sausages yesterday, so carry the water in which I boiled them to the trough." Little Red Riding Hood made sure the great trough was quite full. Then the smell of the sausages reached the wolf, and he sniffed and peeped down, and at last stretched out his neck so far that he could no longer keep his footing and began to slip, and slipped down from the roof straight into the great trough and was drowned. So Little Red Riding Hood went joyously home, and no one ever did anything to harm her again.

# OLD SULTAN

A shepherd had a faithful dog, called Sultan, who was grown very old, and had lost all his teeth. And one day the shepherd said, "I will shoot old Sultan tomorrow morning, for he is of no use now."

But his wife said, "Pray let the poor faithful creature live; he has served us well a great many years, and we ought to give him a livelihood for the rest of his days."

"But what can we do with him?" said the shepherd, "he has not a tooth in his head, and the thieves don't fear him at all; to be sure he has served us, but then he did it to earn his livelihood; tomorrow shall be his last day, depend upon it."

Poor Sultan, who was lying close by them, heard all that the shepherd and his wife said to one another, and was very much frightened to think tomorrow would be his last day; so in the evening he went to his good friend the wolf, who lived in the wood, and told him all his sorrows, and how his master meant to kill him in the morning. "Make yourself easy," said the wolf, "I will give you some good advice. Your master, you know, goes out every morning very early with his wife into the field; and they take their little child with them, and lay it down behind the hedge in the shade while they are at work. Now do you lie down close by the child, and pretend to be watching it, and I will come out of the wood and run away with it; you must run after me as fast as you can, and I will let it drop; then you may carry it back, and they will think you have saved their child, and will be so thankful to you that they will take care of you as long as you live."

The dog liked this plan very well; and accordingly so it was managed. The wolf ran with the child a little way; the shepherd and his wife screamed out; but Sultan soon overtook him, and carried the poor little thing back to his master and mistress.

Then the shepherd patted him on the head, and said, "Old Sultan has saved our child from the wolf, and therefore he shall live and be well taken care of, and have plenty to eat. Wife, go home, and give him a good dinner, and let him have my old cushion to sleep on as long as he lives." So from this time forward Sultan had all that he could wish for.

Soon afterwards the wolf came and wished him joy, and said, "Now, my good fellow, you must tell no tales, but turn your head the other way when I want to taste one of the old shepherd's fine fat sheep."

"No," said Sultan; "I will be true to my master." However, the wolf thought he was jesting, and came one night to get a dainty morsel. But Sultan had told his master what the wolf meant to do; so he lay in wait for him behind the barn door, and when the wolf was busy looking out for a good fat sheep, he had a stout cudgel laid about his back that combed his locks for him finely.

Then the wolf was very angry, and called Sultan "an old rogue," and swore he would have his revenge. So the next morning the wolf sent the boar to challenge Sultan to come into the wood to fight the matter. Now Sultan had nobody he could ask to be his second but the shepherd's old three-legged cat; so he took her with him, and as the poor thing limped along with some trouble, she stuck her tail straight up in the air.

The wolf and the wild boar were first on the ground; and when they espied their enemies coming, and saw the cat's long tail standing straight in the air, they thought she was carrying a sword for Sultan to fight with; and every time she limped, they thought she was picking up a stone to throw at them; so they said they should not like this way of fighting, and the boar lay down behind a bush, and the wolf jumped up into a tree. Sultan and the cat soon came up, and looked about and wondered that no one was there. The boar, however, had not quite hidden himself, for his ears stuck out of the bush; and when he shook one of them a little, the cat, seeing something move, and thinking it was a mouse, sprang upon it, and bit and scratched it, so that the boar jumped up and grunted, and ran away, roaring out, "Look up in the tree, there sits the one who is to blame." So they looked up, and espied the wolf sitting among the branches; and they called him a cowardly rascal, and would not suffer him to come down till he was heartily ashamed of himself, and had promised to be good friends again with old Sultan.

*In a village dwelt a poor old woman who had gathered a bundle of beans.*

# THE STRAW, THE COAL, AND THE BEAN

In a village dwelt a poor old woman who had gathered together a bundle of beans and wanted to cook them. So she made a fire on her hearth, and that it might burn the quicker, she lighted it with a handful of straw. When she was emptying the beans into the pan, one dropped without her observing it, and lay on the ground beside a straw, and soon afterwards a burning coal from the fire leapt down to the two.

Then the straw began and said: "Dear friends, from whence do you come here?"

The coal replied: "I fortunately sprang out of the fire, and if I had not escaped by sheer force, my death would have been certain—I should have been burnt to ashes."

The bean said: "I too have escaped with a whole skin, but if the old woman had got me into the pan, I should have been made into broth without any mercy, like my comrades."

"And would a better fate have fallen to my lot?" said the straw. "The old woman has destroyed all my brethren in fire and smoke; she seized sixty of them at once, and took their lives. I luckily slipped through her fingers."

"But what are we to do now?" said the coal.

"I think," answered the bean, "that as we have so fortunately escaped death, we should keep together like good companions, and lest a new mischance should overtake us here, we should go away together, and repair to a foreign country."

The proposition pleased the two others, and they set out on their way together. Soon, however, they came to a little brook, and as there was no bridge or foot-plank, they did not know how they were to get over it. The straw hit on a good idea, and said: "I will lay myself straight across, and then you can walk over on me as on a bridge."

The straw therefore stretched herself from one bank to the other, and the coal, who was of an impetuous disposition, tripped quite boldly onto the newly built bridge. But when she had reached the middle, and heard the water rushing beneath her, she was, after all, afraid, and stood still, and ventured no farther. The straw, however, began to burn, broke in two pieces, and fell into the stream. The coal slipped after her, hissed when she got into the water, and breathed her last.

The bean, who had prudently stayed behind on the shore, could not but laugh at the event, was unable to stop, and laughed so heartily that she burst. It would have been all over with her, likewise, if, by good fortune, a tailor who was traveling in search of work had not sat down to rest by the brook. As he had a compassionate heart, he pulled out his needle and thread and sewed her together. The bean thanked him most prettily, but as the tailor used black thread, all beans since then have a black seam.

# THE SLEEPING BEAUTY

A king and queen once upon a time reigned in a country a great way off, where there were in those days fairies. Now this king and queen had plenty of money, and plenty of fine clothes to wear, and plenty of good things to eat and drink, and a coach to ride out in every day; but though they had been married many years they had no children, and this grieved them very much indeed. But one day, as the queen was walking by the side of the river at the bottom of the garden, she saw a poor little fish that had thrown itself out of the water and lay gasping and nearly dead on the bank. Then the queen took pity on the little fish, and threw it back again into the river; and before it swam away it lifted its head out of the water and said, "I know what your wish is, and it shall be fulfilled, in return for your kindness to me—you will soon have a daughter."

What the little fish had foretold soon came to pass: the queen had a little girl, so very beautiful that the king could not cease looking on her for joy, and said he would hold a great feast and make merry, and show the child to all the land. So he asked his kinsmen, and nobles, and friends, and neighbors.

But the queen said, "I will have the fairies also, that they might be kind and good to our little daughter."

Now there were thirteen fairies in the kingdom; but as the king and queen had only twelve golden dishes for them

*The king could not cease looking on her for joy.*

to eat out of, they were forced to leave one of the fairies without asking her. So twelve fairies came, each with a high red cap on her head, and red shoes with high heels on her feet, and a long white wand in her hand; and after the feast was over they gathered round in a ring and gave all their best gifts to the little princess. One gave her goodness, another beauty, another riches, and so on till she had all that was good in the world.

Just as eleven of them had done blessing her, a great noise was heard in the courtyard, and word was brought that the thirteenth fairy was come, with a black cap on her head, and black shoes on her feet, and a broomstick in her hand: and presently up she came into the dining hall. Now, as she had not been asked to the feast she was very angry, and scolded the king and queen very much, and set to work to take her revenge. So she cried out, "The king's daughter shall, in her fifteenth year, be wounded by a spindle, and fall down dead."

Then the twelfth of the friendly fairies, who had not yet given her gift, came forward, and said that the evil wish must be fulfilled, but that she could soften its mischief; so her gift was that the king's daughter, when the spindle wounded her, should not really die, but should only fall asleep for a hundred years.

However, the king hoped still to save his dear child altogether from the threatened evil; so he ordered that all the spindles in the kingdom should be bought up and burnt. All the gifts of the first eleven fairies were in the meantime fulfilled; for the princess was so beautiful, and well behaved, and good, and wise, that everyone who knew her loved her.

It happened that, on the very day she was fifteen years old, the king and queen were not at home, and she was left alone in the palace. So she roved about by herself, and looked at all the rooms and chambers, till at last she came to an old tower, up which there was a narrow staircase ending with a little door. In the door there was a golden key, and when she turned it the door sprang open and there sat an old lady spinning away very busily. "Why, how now, good mother," said the princess; "what are you doing there?"

"Spinning," said the old lady, and nodded her head, humming a tune, while buzz! went the wheel.

"How prettily that little thing turns round!" said the princess, and took the spindle and began to try to spin. But scarcely had she touched it, before the fairy's prophecy was fulfilled; the spindle wounded her, and she fell down lifeless on the ground.

However, she was not dead, but had only fallen into a deep sleep; and the king and the queen, who had just come home, and all their court, fell asleep too; and the horses slept in the stables, and the dogs in the court, the pigeons on the housetop, and the very flies slept upon the walls. Even the fire on the hearth left off blazing, and went to sleep; the jack stopped, and the spit that was turning about with a goose upon it for the king's dinner stood still; and the cook, who was at that moment pulling the kitchen boy by the hair to give him a box on the ear for something he had done amiss, let him go, and both fell asleep; the butler, who was slyly tasting the ale, fell asleep with the jug at his lips: and thus everything stood still, and slept soundly.

A large hedge of thorns soon grew round the palace, and every year it became higher and thicker; till at last the old palace was surrounded and hidden, so that not even the roof or the chimneys could be seen. But there went a report through all the land of the beautiful sleeping Briar Rose (for so the king's daughter was called), so that, from time to time, several kings' sons came, and tried to break through the thicket into the palace. This, however, none of them could ever do; for the thorns and bushes laid hold of them, as it were with hands; and there they stuck fast, and died wretchedly.

After many, many years there came a king's son into that land, and an old man told him the story of the thicket of thorns: how a beautiful palace stood behind it, and how a wonderful princess, called Briar Rose, lay in it asleep, with all her court. He told, too, how he had

*The old man tried to hinder him, but he was bent upon going.*

heard from his grandfather that many, many princes had come, and had tried to break through the thicket, but that they had all stuck fast in it, and died.

Then the young prince said, "All this does not frighten me; I will go and see this Briar Rose." The old man tried to hinder him, but he was bent upon going.

Now that very day the hundred years were ended; and as the prince came to the thicket he saw nothing but beautiful flowering shrubs, through which he went with ease, and they shut in after him as thick as ever. Then he came at last to the palace, and there in the court lay the dogs asleep; and the horses were standing in the stables; and on the roof sat the pigeons fast asleep, with their heads under their wings. And when he came into the palace, the flies were sleeping on the walls; the spit was standing still; the butler had the jug of ale at his lips, going to drink a draught; the maid sat with a fowl in her lap ready to be plucked; and the cook in the kitchen was still holding up her hand, as if she was going to strike the boy.

Then he went in farther, and all was so still that he could hear every breath he drew, till at last he came to the old tower, and opened the door of the little room in which Briar Rose was; and there she lay, fast asleep on a couch by the window. She looked so beautiful that he could not take his eyes off her, so he stooped down and gave her a kiss.

And the moment he kissed her she opened her eyes and awoke, and smiled upon him; and they went out together; and soon the king and queen also awoke, and all the court, and gazed on each other with great wonder. And the horses shook themselves, and the dogs jumped up and barked; the pigeons took their heads from under their wings, and looked about and flew into the fields; the flies on the

walls buzzed again; the fire in the kitchen blazed up; round went the jack, and round went the spit, with the goose for the king's dinner upon it; the butler finished his draught of ale; the maid went on plucking the fowl; and the cook gave the boy the box on his ear.

And then the prince and Briar Rose were married, and the wedding feast was given; and they lived happily together all their lives long.

# TOM THUMB

A poor woodman sat in his cottage one night, smoking his pipe by the fireside, while his wife sat by his side spinning. "How lonely it is, wife," said he, as he puffed out a long curl of smoke, "for you and me to sit here by ourselves, without any children to play about and amuse us, while other people seem so happy and merry with their children!"

"What you say is very true," said the wife, sighing, and turning round her wheel; "how happy should I be if I had but one child! If it were ever so small—nay, if it were no bigger than my thumb—I should be very happy, and love it dearly." Now—odd as you may think it—it came to pass that this good woman's wish was fulfilled, just in the very way she had wished it; for, not long afterwards, she had a little boy, who was quite healthy and strong, but was not much bigger than my thumb. So they said, "Well, we cannot say we have not got what we wished for, and, little as he is, we will love him dearly." And they called him Thomas Thumb.

They gave him plenty of food, yet for all they could do he never grew bigger, but kept just the same size as he had been when he was born. Still, his eyes were sharp and sparkling, and he soon showed himself to be a clever little fellow, who always knew well what he was about.

One day, as the woodman was getting ready to go into the wood to cut fuel, he said, "I wish I had someone to bring the cart after me, for I want to make haste."

"Oh, father," cried Tom, "I will take care of that; the cart shall be in the wood by the time you want it."

Then the woodman laughed, and said, "How can that be? You cannot reach up to the horse's bridle."

"Never mind that, father," said Tom; "if my mother will only harness the horse, I will get into his ear and tell him which way to go."

"Well," said the father, "we will try for once."

When the time came the mother harnessed the horse to the cart, and put Tom into his ear; and as he sat there the little man told the beast how to go, crying out, "Go on!" and "Stop!" as he wanted, and thus the horse went on just as well as if the woodman had driven it himself into the wood.

It happened that as the horse was going a little too fast, and Tom was calling out, "Gently! Gently!" two strangers came up.

"What an odd thing that is!" said one. "There is a cart going along, and I hear a carter talking to the horse, but yet I can see no one."

"That is queer, indeed," said the other; "let us follow the cart, and see where it goes."

So they went on into the wood, till at last they came to the place where the woodman was. Then Tom Thumb, seeing his father, cried out, "See, father, here I am with the cart, all safe and sound! Now take me down!" So his father took hold of the horse with one hand, and with the other took his son out of the horse's ear, and put him down upon a straw, where he sat as merry as you please.

The two strangers were all this time looking on, and did not know what to say for wonder. At last one took the other aside, and said, "That little urchin will make our fortune, if we can get him and carry him about from town to town as a show; we must buy him." So they went up to the woodman and asked him what he would take for the little man.

"He will be better off," said they, "with us than with you."

"I won't sell him at all," said the father; "my own flesh and blood is dearer to me than all the silver and gold in the world."

But Tom, hearing of the bargain they wanted to make, crept up his father's coat to his shoulder and whispered in his ear, "Take the money, father, and let them have me; I'll soon come back to you."

So the woodman at last said he would sell Tom to the strangers for a large piece of gold, and they paid the price.

"Where would you like to sit?" said one of them.

"Oh, put me on the rim of your hat; that will be a nice gallery for me; I can walk about there and see the country as we go along."

So they did as he wished; and when Tom had taken leave of his father they took him away with them.

They journeyed on till it began to be dusk, and then the little man said, "Let me get down, I'm tired."

So the man took off his hat, and put him down on a clod of earth in a plowed field by the side of the road. But Tom ran about among the furrows, and at last slipped into an old mouse hole. "Good night, my masters!" said he, "I'm off! Mind and look sharp after me the next time."

Then they ran at once to the place, and poked the ends of their sticks into the mouse hole, but all in vain; Tom only crawled farther and farther in; and at last it became quite dark, so that they were forced to go their way without their prize, as sulky as could be.

When Tom found they were gone, he came out of his hiding place. "What dangerous walking it is," said he, "in this plowed field! If I were to fall from one of these great clods, I should undoubtedly break my neck."

At last, by good luck, he found a large empty snail shell. "This is lucky," said he, "I can sleep here very well"; and in he crept.

Just as he was falling asleep, he heard two men passing by, chatting together; and one said to the other, "How can we rob that rich parson's house of his silver and gold?"

"I'll tell you!" cried Tom.

"What noise was that?" said the thief, frightened; "I'm sure I heard someone speak."

*"Oh, put me on the rim of your hat; that will be a nice gallery for me;
I can walk about there and see the country as we go along."*

They stood still listening, and Tom said, "Take me with you, and I'll soon show you how to get the parson's money."

"But where are you?" said they.

"Look about on the ground," answered he, "and listen where the sound comes from."

At last the thieves found him out, and lifted him up in their hands. "You little urchin!" they said, "what can you do for us?"

"Why, I can get between the iron window bars of the parson's house, and throw you out whatever you want."

"That's a good thought," said the thieves; "come along, we shall see what you can do."

When they came to the parson's house, Tom slipped through the window bars into the room, and then called out as loud as he could bawl, "Will you have all that is here?"

At this the thieves were frightened, and said, "Softly, softly! Speak low, that you may not awaken anybody."

But Tom seemed as if he did not understand them, and bawled out again, "How much will you have? Shall I throw it all out?"

Now the cook lay in the next room; and hearing a noise she raised herself up in her bed and listened.

Meantime the thieves were frightened, and ran off a little way; but at last they plucked up their hearts, and said, "The little urchin is only trying to make fools of us." So they came back and whispered softly to him, saying, "Now let us have no more of your roguish jokes; but throw us out some of the money."

Then Tom called out as loud as he could, "Very well! Hold your hands! Here it comes."

The cook heard this quite plain, so she sprang out of bed, and ran to open the door. The thieves ran off as if a wolf was at their tails, while the cook, having groped about and found nothing, went away for a light. By the time she came back, Tom had slipped off into the barn; and when she had looked about and searched every hole and corner, and found nobody, she went to bed, thinking she must have been dreaming with her eyes open.

The little man crawled about in the hayloft, and at last found a snug place to finish his night's rest in; so he laid himself down, meaning to sleep till daylight and then find his way home to his father and mother. But alas! how woefully he was undone! What crosses and sorrows happen to us all in this world! The cook got up early, before daybreak, to feed the cows; and going straight to the hayloft, carried away a large bundle of hay, with the little man in the middle of it, fast asleep. He still, however, slept on, and did not awake till he found himself in the mouth of the cow; for the cook had put the hay into the cow's rick, and the cow had taken Tom up in a mouthful of it.

"Good lack-a-day!" said he, "how came I to tumble into the mill?" But he soon found out where he really was; and was forced to have all his wits about him, that he might not get between the cow's teeth, and so be crushed to death.

At last down he went into her stomach.

"It is rather dark," said he; "they forgot to build windows in this room to let the sun in; a candle would be no bad thing." Though he made the best of his bad luck, he did not like his quarters at all; and the worst of it was that more and more hay was always coming down, and the space left for him became smaller and smaller. At last he cried out as loud as he could, "Don't bring me any more hay! Don't bring me any more hay!"

The cook happened to be just then milking the cow; and hearing someone speak, but seeing nobody, and yet being quite sure it was the same voice that she had heard in the night, she was so frightened that she fell off her stool, and overset the milk pail. As soon as she could pick herself up out of the dirt, she ran off as fast as she could to her master the parson, and said, "Sir, sir, the cow is talking!"

But the parson said, "Woman, you are surely mad!" However, he went with her into the cow house, to try and see what was the matter.

Scarcely had they set foot on the threshold, when Tom called out, "Don't bring me any more hay!"

Then the parson himself was frightened, and thinking the cow was surely bewitched, told his man to kill her on the spot. So the cow was killed, and cut up; and the stomach, in which Tom lay, was thrown out upon a dunghill.

Tom soon set himself to work to get out, which was not a very easy task; but at last, just as he had made room to get his head out, fresh ill luck befell him. A hungry wolf sprang out, and swallowed up the whole stomach, with Tom in it, at one gulp, and ran away.

Tom, however, was still not disheartened; and thinking the wolf would not dislike having some chat with him as he was going along, he called out, "My good friend, I can show you a famous treat."

"Where's that?" said the wolf.

"In such and such a house," said Tom, describing his own father's house. "You can crawl through the drain into the kitchen and then into the pantry, and there you will find cakes, ham, beef, cold chicken, roast pig, apple dumplings, and everything that your heart can desire."

The wolf did not need to be asked twice; so that very night he went to the house and crawled through the drain into the kitchen, and then into the pantry, and ate and drank there to his heart's content. As soon as he had had enough he wanted to get away; but he had eaten so much that he could not go out by the same way he came in. This was just what Tom had reckoned upon; and now he began to set up a great shout, making all the noise he could.

"Will you be easy?" said the wolf; "you'll awaken everybody in the house if you make such a clatter."

"What's that to me?" said the little man. "You have had your frolic, now I've a mind to be merry myself"; and he began, singing and shouting as loud as he could.

The woodman and his wife, being awakened by the noise, peeped through a crack in the door; but when they saw a wolf was there, you may well suppose that they were sadly frightened; and the woodman ran for his axe, and gave his wife a scythe. "Do you stand behind me," said the woodman, "and when I have knocked him on the head you must rip him up with the scythe."

Tom heard all this, and cried out, "Father, father! I am here, the wolf has swallowed me."

And his father said, "Heaven be praised! We have found our dear child again"; and he told his wife not to use the scythe for fear she should hurt him. Then he aimed a great blow, and struck the wolf on the head, and killed him on the spot! And when he was dead they cut open his body and set Tommy free. "Ah!" said the father, "what fears we have had for you!"

"Yes, father," answered he; "I have traveled all over the world, I think, in one way or other, since we parted; and now I am very glad to come home and get fresh air again."

"Why, where have you been?" said his father.

"I have been in a mouse hole—and in a snail shell—and down a cow's throat—and in the wolf's belly; and yet here I am again, safe and sound."

"Well," said they, "you are come back, and we will not sell you again for all the riches in the world."

Then they hugged and kissed their dear little son, and gave him plenty to eat and drink, for he was very hungry; and then they fetched new clothes for him, for his old ones had been quite spoiled on his journey. So Master Thumb stayed at home with his father and mother, in peace; for though he had been so great a traveler, and had done and seen so many fine things, and was fond enough of telling the whole story, he always agreed that, after all, there's no place like home!

# THE TWELVE DANCING PRINCESSES

There was a king who had twelve beautiful daughters. They slept in twelve beds all in one room; and when they went to bed, the doors were shut and locked up; but every morning their shoes were found to be quite worn through as if they had been danced in all night; and yet nobody could find out how it happened, or where they had been.

Then the king made it known to all the land that if any man could discover the secret, and find out where it was that the princesses danced in the night, he should have the one he liked best for his wife, and should be king after his death; but whoever tried and did not succeed, after three days and nights should be put to death.

A king's son soon came. He was well entertained, and in the evening was taken to the chamber next to the one where the princesses lay in their twelve beds. There he was to sit and watch where they went to dance; and, in order that nothing might pass without his hearing it, the door of his chamber was left open. But the king's son soon fell asleep; and when he awoke in the morning he found that the princesses had all been dancing, for the soles of their shoes were full of holes. The same thing happened the second and third night, so the king ordered his head to be cut off. After him came several others; but they had all the same luck, and all lost their lives in the same manner.

Now it chanced that an old soldier, who had been wounded in battle and could fight no longer, passed through the country where this king reigned, and as he was traveling through a wood, he met an old woman, who asked him where he was going. "I hardly know where I am going, or what I had better do," said the soldier; "but I think I should like very well to find out where it is that the princesses dance, and then in time I might be a king."

"Well," said the old dame, "that is no very hard task, only take care not to drink any of the wine which one of the princesses will bring to you in the evening; and as soon as she leaves, you pretend to be fast asleep." Then she gave him a cloak, and said, "As soon as you put that on you will become invisible, and you will then be able to follow the princesses wherever they go."

When the soldier heard all this good counsel, he determined to try his luck: so he went to the king, and said he was willing to undertake the task. He was as well received as the others had been, and the king ordered fine royal robes to be given him; and when the evening came he was led to the outer chamber. Just as he was going to lie down, the eldest of the princesses brought him a cup of wine; but the soldier threw it all away secretly, taking care not to drink a drop. Then he laid himself down on his bed, and in a little while began to snore very loud as if he was fast asleep.

When the twelve princesses heard this they laughed heartily; and the eldest said, "This fellow too might have done a wiser thing than lose his life in this way!"

Then they rose up and opened their drawers and boxes, and took out all their fine clothes, and dressed themselves at the glass, and skipped about as if they were eager to begin dancing. But the youngest said, "I don't know why it is, but while you are all so happy I feel very uneasy; I am sure some mischance will befall us."

"You simpleton," said the eldest, "you are always afraid; have you forgotten how many kings' sons have already watched in vain? And as for this soldier, even if I had not given him his sleeping draught, he would have slept soundly enough."

When they were all ready, they went and looked at the soldier; but he snored on, and did not stir hand or foot, so they thought they were quite safe; and the eldest went up to her own bed and clapped her hands, and the bed sank into the floor and a trapdoor flew open. The soldier saw them going down through the trapdoor one after another, the eldest leading the way; and thinking he had no time to lose, he jumped up, put on the cloak which the old woman had given him, and followed them; but in the middle of the stairs he trod on the gown of the youngest princess, and she cried out to her sisters, "All is not right; someone took hold of my gown."

"You silly creature!" said the eldest, "it is nothing but a nail in the wall."

Then down they all went, and at the bottom they found themselves in a most delightful grove of trees; and the leaves were all of silver, and glittered and sparkled beautifully. The soldier wished to take away some token of the place; so he broke off a little branch, and there came a loud noise from the tree. Then the youngest daughter said again, "I am sure all is not right—did not you hear that noise? That never happened before."

But the eldest said, "It is only our princes, who are shouting for joy at our approach."

Then they came to another grove of trees, where all the leaves were of gold; and afterwards to a third, where the leaves were all glittering diamonds. And the soldier broke a branch from each; and every time there was a loud noise, which made the youngest sister tremble with fear; but the eldest still said, it was only the princes, who were crying for joy. So they went on till they came to a great lake; and at the side of the lake there lay twelve little boats with twelve handsome princes in them, who seemed to be waiting there for the princesses.

One of the princesses went into each boat, and the soldier stepped into the same boat as the youngest. As they were rowing over the lake, the prince who was in the boat with the youngest princess and the soldier said, "I do not know why it is, but though I am rowing with all

my might we do not get on so fast as usual, and I am quite tired: the boat seems very heavy today."

"It is only the heat of the weather," said the princess. "I feel very warm too."

On the other side of the lake stood a fine illuminated castle, from which came the merry music of horns and trumpets. There they all landed, and went into the castle, and each prince danced with his princess; and the soldier, who was all the time invisible, danced with them too; and when any of the princesses had a cup of wine set by her, he drank it all up, so that when she put the cup to her mouth it was empty. At this, too, the youngest sister was terribly frightened, but the eldest always silenced her. They danced on till three o'clock in the morning, and then all their shoes were worn out, so that they were obliged to leave off. The princes rowed them back again over the lake (but this time the soldier placed himself in the boat with the eldest princess); and on the opposite shore they took leave of each other, the princesses promising to come again the next night.

When they came to the stairs, the soldier ran on before the princesses, and laid himself down; and as the twelve sisters slowly came up, very much tired, they heard him snoring in his bed; so they said, "Now all is quite safe"; then they undressed themselves, put away their fine clothes, pulled off their shoes, and went to bed. In the morning the soldier said nothing about what had happened, but determined to see more of this strange adventure, and went again the second and third night; and everything happened just as before; the princesses danced each time till their shoes were worn to pieces, and then returned home. However, on the third night the soldier carried away one of the golden cups as a token of where he had been.

As soon as the time came when he was to declare the secret, he was taken before the king with the three branches and the golden cup; and the twelve princesses stood listening behind the door to hear what he would say. And when the king asked him, "Where do my twelve daughters dance at night?" he answered, "With twelve princes in a castle underground." And then he told the king all that had happened, and showed him the three branches and the golden cup which he had brought with him. Then the king called for the princesses, and asked them whether what the soldier said was true; and when they saw that they were discovered, and that it was of no use to deny what had happened, they confessed it all. And the king asked the soldier which of them he would choose for his wife; and he answered, "I am not very young, so I will have the eldest." And they were married that very day, and the soldier was chosen to be the king's heir.

# THE FISHERMAN AND HIS WIFE

There was once a fisherman who lived with his wife in a pigsty, close by the seaside. The fisherman used to go out fishing all day long, and one day, as he sat on the shore with his rod, looking at the sparkling waves and watching his line, all of a sudden his float was dragged away deep into the water, and in drawing it up he pulled out a great fish.

But the fish said, "Pray let me live! I am not a real fish; I am an enchanted prince. Put me in the water again, and let me go!"

"Oh, ho!" said the man, "you need not make so many words about the matter; I will have nothing to do with a fish that can talk; so swim away, sir, as soon as you please!"

Then he put him back into the water, and the fish darted straight down to the bottom, and left a long streak of blood behind him on the wave.

When the fisherman went back home to his wife in the pigsty, he told her how he had caught a great fish, and how it had told him that it was an enchanted prince, and how, on hearing it speak, he had let it go again.

"Did you not ask it for anything?" said the wife. "We live very wretchedly here, in this nasty dirty pigsty; do go back and tell the fish we want a snug little cottage."

The fisherman did not much like the business: however, he went back to the seashore; and when he got there the water looked all yellow and green. And he stood at the water's edge, and said:

*"O man of the sea!*
*Hearken to me!*
*My wife Ilsabill*
*Will have her own will,*
*And hath sent me to beg a boon of thee!"*

Then the fish came swimming to him, and said, "Well, what is her will? What does your wife want?"

"Ah!" said the fisherman, "she says that when I had caught you, I ought to have asked you for something before I let you go; she does not like living any longer in the pigsty, and wants a snug little cottage."

"Go home, then," said the fish; "she is in the cottage already!" So the man went home, and saw his wife standing at the door of a nice trim little cottage.

"Come in, come in!" said she. "Is not this much better than the filthy pigsty we had?" And there was a parlor, and a bedchamber, and a kitchen; and behind the cottage there was a little garden, planted with all sorts of flowers and fruits; and there was a courtyard behind, full of ducks and chickens.

"Ah!" said the fisherman, "how happily we shall live now!"

"We will try to do so, at least," said his wife.

Everything went right for a week or two, and then Dame Ilsabill said, "Husband, there is not nearly room enough for us in this cottage; the courtyard and the garden are a great deal too small; I should like to have a large stone castle to live in. Go to the fish again and tell him to give us a castle."

"Wife," said the fisherman, "I don't like to go to him again, for perhaps he will be angry; we ought to be content with this pretty cottage."

"Nonsense!" said the wife; "he will do it very willingly, I know. Go along and try!"

The fisherman went, but his heart was very heavy: and when he came to the sea, it looked blue and gloomy, though it was very calm; and he went close to the edge of the waves, and said:

*"O man of the sea!*
*Hearken to me!*
*My wife Ilsabill*
*Will have her own will,*
*And hath sent me to beg a boon of thee!"*

"Well, what does she want now?" said the fish.

"Ah!" said the man, dolefully, "my wife wants to live in a stone castle."

"Go home, then," said the fish; "she is standing at the gate of it already."

So away went the fisherman, and found his wife standing before the gate of a great castle. "See," said she, "is not this grand?"

With that they went into the castle together, and found a great many servants there, and the rooms all richly furnished, and full of golden chairs and tables; and behind the castle was a garden, and around it was a park half a mile long, full of sheep, and goats, and hares, and deer; and in the courtyard were stables and cow houses.

"Well," said the man, "now we will live cheerful and happy in this beautiful castle for the rest of our lives."

"Perhaps we may," said the wife; "but let us sleep upon it, before we make up our minds to that." So they went to bed.

The next morning when Dame Ilsabill awoke it was broad daylight, and she jogged the fisherman with her elbow, and said, "Get up, husband, and bestir yourself, for we must be king of all the land."

"Wife, wife," said the man, "why should we wish to be the king? I will not be king."

"Then I will," said she.

"But, wife," said the fisherman, "how can you be king—the fish cannot make you a king!"

"Husband," said she, "say no more about it, but go and try! I will be king."

So the man went away quite sorrowful to think that his wife should want to be king. This time the sea looked a dark gray color, and was overspread with curling waves with ridges of foam as he cried out:

*"O man of the sea!*
*Hearken to me!*
*My wife Ilsabill*
*Will have her own will,*
*And hath sent me to beg a boon of thee!"*

"Well, what would she have now?" said the fish.

"Alas!" said the poor man, "my wife wants to be king."

"Go home," said the fish; "she is king already."

Then the fisherman went home; and as he came close to the palace he saw a troop of soldiers, and heard the sound of drums and trumpets. And when he went in he saw his wife sitting on a throne of gold and diamonds, with a golden crown upon her head; and on each side of her stood six fair maidens, each a head taller than the other. "Well, wife," said the fisherman, "are you king?"

"Yes," said she, "I am king."

And when he had looked at her for a long time, he said, "Ah, wife! What a fine thing it is to be king! Now we shall never have anything more to wish for as long as we live."

"I don't know how that may be," said she. "Never is a long time. I am king, it is true; but I begin to be tired of that, and I think I should like to be emperor."

"Alas, wife! Why should you wish to be emperor?" said the fisherman.

"Husband," said she, "go to the fish! I say I will be emperor."

"Ah, wife!" replied the fisherman, "the fish cannot make an emperor, I am sure, and I should not like to ask him for such a thing."

"I am king," said Ilsabill, "and you are my slave; so go at once!"

So the fisherman was forced to go; and he muttered as he went along, "This will come to no good, it is too much to ask; the fish will be tired at last, and then we shall be sorry for what we have done."

He soon came to the seashore; and the water was quite black and muddy, and a mighty whirlwind blew over the waves and rolled them about, but he went as near as he could to the water's brink, and said:

> *"O man of the sea!*
> *Hearken to me!*
> *My wife Ilsabill*
> *Will have her own will,*
> *And hath sent me to beg a boon of thee!"*

"What would she have now?" said the fish.

"Ah!" said the fisherman, "she wants to be emperor."

"Go home," said the fish; "she is emperor already."

So he went home again; and as he came near he saw his wife Ilsabill sitting on a very lofty throne made of solid gold, with a great crown on her head full two yards high; and on each side of her stood her guards and attendants in a row, each one smaller than the other, from the tallest giant down to a little dwarf no bigger than my finger. And before her stood princes, and dukes, and earls; and the fisherman went up to her and said, "Wife, are you emperor?"

"Yes," said she, "I am emperor."

"Ah!" said the man, as he gazed upon her, "what a fine thing it is to be emperor!"

"Husband," said she, "why should we stop at being emperor? I will be pope next."

"O wife, wife!" said he, "how can you be pope? There is but one pope at a time in Christendom."

"Husband," said she, "I will be pope this very day."

"But," replied the husband, "the fish cannot make you pope."

"What nonsense!" said she; "if he can make an emperor, he can make a pope. Go and try him."

So the fisherman went. But when he came to the shore the wind was raging and the sea was tossed up and down in boiling waves, and the ships were in trouble, and rolled fearfully upon the tops of the billows. In the middle of the heavens there was a little piece of blue sky, but towards the south all was red, as if a dreadful storm was rising. At this sight the fisherman was dreadfully frightened, and he trembled so that his knees knocked together, but still he went down near to the shore, and said:

> *"O man of the sea!*
> *Hearken to me!*
> *My wife Ilsabill*
> *Will have her own will,*
> *And hath sent me to beg a boon of thee!"*

"What does she want now?" said the fish.

"Ah!" said the fisherman, "my wife wants to be pope."

"Go home," said the fish; "she is pope already."

Then the fisherman went home, and found Ilsabill sitting on a throne that was two miles high. And she had three great crowns on her head, and around her stood all the pomp and power of the Church. And on each side of her were two rows of burning lights, of all sizes, the greatest as large as the highest and biggest tower in the world, and the least no larger than a small rushlight.

"Wife," said the fisherman, as he looked at all this greatness, "are you pope?"

"Yes," said she, "I am pope."

"Well, wife," replied he, "it is a grand thing to be pope; and now you must be content, for you can be nothing greater."

"I will think about that," said the wife.

Then they went to bed, but Dame Ilsabill could not sleep all night for thinking what she should be next. At last, just as she was falling asleep, morning broke and the sun rose. "Ha!" thought she, as she woke up and looked at it through the window, "after all I cannot prevent the sun rising."

At this thought she was very angry, and wakened her husband, and said, "Husband, go to the fish and tell him I must be lord of the sun and moon."

The fisherman was half asleep, but the thought frightened him so much that he started and fell out of bed. "Alas, wife!" said he, "can you not be content with being pope?"

"No," said she, "I am very uneasy as long as the sun and moon rise without my leave. Go to the fish at once!"

Then the man went shivering with fear; and as he was going down to the shore a dreadful storm arose, so that the trees and the very rocks shook. And all the heavens became black with stormy clouds, and the lightning played and the thunder rolled; and you might have seen in

the sea great black waves, swelling up like mountains with crowns of white foam upon their heads. And the fisherman crept towards the sea, and cried out, as well as he could:

> *"O man of the sea!*
> *Hearken to me!*
> *My wife Ilsabill*
> *Will have her own will,*
> *And hath sent me to beg a boon of thee!"*

"What does she want now?" said the fish.
"Ah!" said he, "she wants to be lord of the sun and moon."
"Go home," said the fish, "to your pigsty again."
And there they live to this very day.

# THE GOOSE GIRL

The king of a great land died, and left his queen to take care of their only child. This child was a daughter, who was very beautiful; and her mother loved her dearly, and was very kind to her. And there was a good fairy too, who was fond of the princess, and helped her mother to watch over her. When she grew up, she was betrothed to a prince who lived a great way off; and as the time drew near for her to be married, she got ready to set off on her journey to his country. Then the queen her mother packed up a great many costly things: jewels, and gold, and silver; trinkets, and fine dresses, and in short everything that became a royal bride. And she gave her a waiting-maid to ride with her and give her into the bridegroom's hands; and each had a horse for the journey. Now the princess's horse was the fairy's gift, and it was called Falada, and could speak.

When the time came for them to set out, the fairy went into her bedchamber, and took a little knife, and cut off a lock of her hair, and gave it to the princess, and said, "Take care of it, dear child; for it is a charm that may be of use to you on the road." Then they all took a sorrowful leave of the princess; and she put the lock of hair into her bosom, got upon her horse, and set off on her journey to her bridegroom's kingdom.

One day, as they were riding along by a brook, the princess began to feel very thirsty: and she said to her maid, "Pray get down and fetch me some water in my golden cup out of yonder brook, for I want to drink."

"Nay," said the maid, "if you are thirsty, get off yourself, and stoop down by the water and drink; I shall not be your waiting-maid any longer."

Then she was so thirsty that she got down, and knelt over the little brook, and drank; for she was frightened, and dared not bring out her golden cup; and she wept and said, "Alas! what will become of me?" And the lock answered her, and said:

*"Alas! alas! if thy mother knew it,*
*Sadly, sadly, would she rue it."*

But the princess was very gentle and meek, so she said nothing about her maid's ill behavior, but got upon her horse again.

Then all rode farther on their journey, till the day grew so warm, and the sun so scorching, that the bride began to feel very thirsty again; and at last, when they came to a river, she forgot her maid's previous rude speech, and said, "Pray get down, and fetch me some water to drink in my golden cup."

But the maid answered her, and even spoke even more haughtily than before: "Drink if you will, but I shall not be your waiting-maid."

Then the princess was so thirsty that she got off her horse, and lay down, and held her head over the running stream, and cried and said, "What will become of me?"

And the lock of hair answered her again:

*"Alas! alas! if thy mother knew it,*
*Sadly, sadly, would she rue it."*

And as she leaned down to drink, the lock of hair fell from her bosom, and floated away with the water.

Now she was so frightened that she did not see it; but her maid saw it, and was very glad, for she knew it was a charm; and she saw that the poor bride would be in her power, now that she had lost the hair.

So when the bride had done drinking, and would have got upon Falada again, the maid said, "I shall ride upon Falada, and you may have my horse instead"; so she was forced to give up her horse, and soon afterwards to take off her royal clothes and put on her maid's shabby ones.

At last, as they drew near the end of their journey, this treacherous servant threatened to kill her mistress if she ever told anyone what had happened. But Falada saw it all, and marked it well.

Then the waiting-maid rode on upon Falada, and the real bride rode upon the other horse, and they went on in this way till at last they came to the royal court. There was great joy at their coming, and the prince flew to meet them, and lifted the maid from her horse, thinking she was the one who was to be his wife; and she was led upstairs to the royal chamber; but the true princess was told to stay in the court below.

Now the old king happened just then to have nothing else to do; so he amused himself by sitting at his kitchen window, looking at what was going on; and he saw her in the courtyard. As she looked very pretty, and too delicate for a waiting-maid, he went up into the royal chamber to ask the bride who it was she had brought with her but had thus left standing in the court below.

"I brought her with me for the sake of her company on the road," said she; "pray give the girl some work to do, that she may not be idle."

The old king could not for some time think of any work for her to do; but at last he said, "I have a lad who takes care of my geese; she may go and help him." Now the name of this lad that the real bride was to help in watching the king's geese was Curdken.

But the false bride said to the prince, "Dear husband, pray do me one piece of kindness."

"That I will," said the prince.

"Then tell one of your slaughterers to cut off the head of the horse I rode upon, for it was very unruly, and plagued me sadly on the road." But the truth was, she was very much afraid lest Falada should someday

*"Falada, Falada, there thou hangest!"*

or other speak, and tell all she had done to the princess. She had her way, and the faithful Falada was killed; but when the true princess heard of it, she wept, and begged the man to nail up Falada's head in a large dark gateway of the city, through which she had to pass every morning and evening, that there she might still see him sometimes. Then the slaughterer said he would do as she wished; and cut off the head, and nailed it up in the dark gateway.

Early the next morning, as she and Curdken went out through the gate, she said sorrowfully: "Falada, Falada, there thou hangest!" and the head answered:

> "Bride, bride, there thou gangest!
> Alas! alas! if thy mother knew it,
> Sadly, sadly, would she rue it."

Then they went out of the city, and drove the geese on. And when she came to the meadow, she sat down upon a bank there, and let down her waving locks of hair, which were all of pure silver; and when Curdken saw it glitter in the sun, he ran up, and would have pulled some of the locks out, but she cried:

> "Blow, breezes, blow!
> Let Curdken's hat go!
> Blow, breezes, blow!
> Let him after it go!
> O'er hills, dales, and rocks,
> Away be it whirl'd
> Till the silvery locks
> Are all comb'd and curl'd!"

Then there came a wind so strong that it blew off Curdken's hat; and away it flew over the hills: and he was forced to turn and run after it. By the time he came back, she had done combing and curling her hair, and had put it up again safe. Then he was very angry and sulky, and would not speak to her at all; but they watched the geese until it grew dark in the evening, and then drove them homewards.

The next morning, as they were going through the dark gateway, the poor girl looked up at Falada's head, and cried: "Falada, Falada, there thou hangest!" and the head answered:

> *"Bride, bride, there thou gangest!*
> *Alas! alas! if thy mother knew it,*
> *Sadly, sadly, would she rue it."*

Then she drove on the geese, and sat down again in the meadow, and began to comb out her hair as before; and Curdken ran up to her, and wanted to take hold of it; but she cried out quickly:

> *"Blow, breezes, blow!*
> *Let Curdken's hat go!*
> *Blow, breezes, blow!*
> *Let him after it go!*
> *O'er hills, dales, and rocks,*
> *Away be it whirl'd*
> *Till the silvery locks*
> *Are all comb'd and curl'd!*

Then the wind came and blew away his hat; and off it flew a great way, over the hills and far away, so that he had to run after it; and when he came back she had bound up her hair again, and all was safe. So they watched the geese till it grew dark.

In the evening, after they came home, Curdken went to the old king, and said, "I cannot have that strange girl to help me to keep the geese any longer."

*"Blow, breezes, blow!*
*Let Curdken's hat go!*
*Blow, breezes, blow!*
*Let him after it go!"*

"Why?" said the king.

"Because, instead of doing any good, she does nothing but tease me all day long."

Then the king made him tell him what had happened. And Curdken said, "When we go in the morning through the dark gateway with our flock of geese, she cries and talks with the head of a horse that hangs upon the wall, and says: 'Falada, Falada, there thou hangest!' and the head answers:

> 'Bride, bride, there thou gangest!
> Alas! alas! if thy mother knew it,
> Sadly, sadly, would she rue it.'"

And Curdken went on to tell the king what had happened upon the meadow where the geese fed: how his hat was blown away, and how he was forced to run after it, and to leave his flock of geese to themselves.

The old king told the boy to go out again the next day, and when morning came, he placed himself beside the dark gateway, and heard how she spoke to Falada, and how Falada answered. Then he went into the field, and hid himself in a bush by the meadow's side; and he soon saw with his own eyes how they drove the flock of geese; and how, after a little time, she let down her hair that glittered in the sun. And then he heard her say:

> "Blow, breezes, blow!
> Let Curdken's hat go!
> Blow, breezes, blow!
> Let him after it go!
> O'er hills, dales, and rocks,
> Away be it whirl'd
> Till the silvery locks
> Are all comb'd and curl'd!"

And soon came a gale of wind, and carried away Curdken's hat, and away went Curdken after it, while the girl went on combing and curling her hair. All this the old king saw, and then he went home without being seen. When the little goose girl came back in the evening he called her aside, and asked her why she behaved as she did; she burst into tears, and said, "That I must not tell you or any man, or I shall lose my life."

But the old king begged so hard that she had no peace till she had told him all the tale, from beginning to end, word for word. And it was very lucky for her that she did so, for when she had done the king ordered royal clothes to be put upon her, and gazed on her with wonder, she was so beautiful. Then he called his son and told him that he had only a false bride, one who was merely a waiting-maid, while the true bride stood by. And the young king rejoiced when he saw her beauty, and heard how meek and patient she had been; and without saying anything to the false bride, the king ordered a great feast to be got ready for all his court. The bridegroom sat at the top, with the false princess on one side, and the true one on the other; but nobody recognized her, for her beauty was quite dazzling to their eyes; and she did not seem at all like the little goose girl, now that she had her brilliant dress on.

When they had eaten and drunk, and were very merry, the old king said he would tell them a tale. So he began, and told all the story of the princess, as if it was one that he had once heard; and he asked the true waiting-maid what she thought ought to be done to anyone who would behave thus.

"Nothing better," said this false bride, "than that she should be thrown into a cask stuck round with sharp nails, and that two white horses should be put to it, and should drag it from street to street till she was dead."

"Thou art she!" said the old king; "and as thou hast judged thyself, so shall it be done to thee."

And the young king was then married to his true wife, and they reigned over the kingdom in peace and happiness all their lives; and the good fairy came to see them, and restored the faithful Falada to life again.

*After a little while the frog came up again, with the ball in his mouth.*

# THE FROG PRINCE

One fine evening, a young princess put on her bonnet and clogs, and went out to take a walk by herself in a wood. When she came to a cool spring of water that rose in the midst of it, she sat down to rest a while. Now she had a golden ball in her hand, which was her favorite plaything; and she was always tossing it up into the air, and catching it again as it fell. After a time she threw it up so high that she missed catching it as it fell, and the ball bounded away, and rolled along upon the ground, till at last it fell down into the spring. The princess looked into the spring after her ball, but it was very deep, so deep that she could not see the bottom of it. Then she began to bewail her loss, and said, "Alas! if I could only get my ball again, I would give all my fine clothes and jewels, and everything that I have in the world."

While she was speaking, a frog put his head out of the water, and said, "Princess, why do you weep so bitterly?"

"Alas!" said she, "what can you do for me, you nasty frog? My golden ball has fallen into the spring."

The frog said, "I want not your pearls, and jewels, and fine clothes; but if you will love me, and let me live with you and eat from off your golden plate and sleep upon your bed, I will bring you your ball again."

"What nonsense," thought the princess, "this silly frog is talking! He can never even get out of the spring to visit me, though he may be able to get my ball for me, and therefore I will tell him he shall have what he asks." So she said to the frog, "Well, if you will bring me my ball, I will do all you ask."

Then the frog put his head down, and dived deep under the water; and after a little while he came up again, with the ball in his mouth, and threw it onto the edge of the spring. As soon as the young princess saw her ball, she ran to pick it up; and she was so overjoyed to have it in her hand again, that she never thought of the frog, but ran home with it as fast as she could. The frog called after her, "Stay, princess, and take me with you as you said," but she did not stop to hear a word.

The next day, just as the princess had sat down to dinner, she heard a strange noise—tap, tap—plash, plash—as if something was coming up the marble staircase, and soon afterwards there was a gentle knock at the door, and a little voice cried out and said:

*"Open the door, my princess dear,*
*Open the door to thy true love here!*
*Remember the words that thou and I said*
*By the fountain cool, in the greenwood shade."*

Then the princess ran to the door and opened it, and there she saw the frog, whom she had quite forgotten. At this sight she was sadly frightened, and shutting the door as fast as she could came back to her seat. The king, her father, seeing that something had frightened her, asked her what was the matter. "There is a nasty frog," said she, "at the door, that lifted my ball for me out of the spring last evening. I told him that he should live with me here, thinking that he could never get out of the spring; but there he is at the door, and he wants to come in."

While she was speaking the frog knocked again at the door, and said:

*"Open the door, my princess dear,*
*Open the door to thy true love here!*
*Remember the words that thou and I said*
*By the fountain cool, in the greenwood shade."*

Then the king said to the young princess, "As you have given your word you must keep it; so go and let him in."

She did so, and the frog hopped into the room, and then straight on—tap, tap—plash, plash—from the bottom of the room to the top, till he came up close to the table where the princess sat. "Pray lift me upon your chair," said he to the princess, "and let me sit next to you."

As soon as she had done this, the frog said, "Put your plate nearer to me, that I may eat from it." This she did, and when he had eaten as much as he could, he said, "Now I am tired; carry me upstairs, and put me into your bed." And the princess, though very unwilling, took him up in her hand, and put him upon the pillow of her own bed, where he slept all night long.

As soon as it was light he jumped up, hopped downstairs, and went out of the house. "Now, then," thought the princess, "at last he is gone, and I shall be troubled with him no more."

But she was mistaken; for when night came again she heard the same tapping at the door; and the frog came once more, and said:

> *"Open the door, my princess dear,*
> *Open the door to thy true love here!*
> *Remember the words that thou and I said*
> *By the fountain cool, in the greenwood shade."*

And when the princess opened the door the frog came in, ate with her, and slept upon her pillow as before, till the morning broke. And the third night he did the same.

But when the princess awoke on the following morning she was astonished to see, instead of the frog, a handsome prince, gazing on her with the most beautiful eyes she had ever seen, and standing at the head of her bed.

He told her that he had been enchanted by a spiteful fairy, who had changed him into a frog; and that he had been fated so to abide

*And the princess, though very unwilling, took him up in her hand.*

till some princess should take him out of the spring, and let him eat from her plate, and sleep upon her bed for three nights. "You," said the prince, "have broken his cruel charm, and now I have nothing to wish for but that you should go with me into my father's kingdom, where I will marry you, and love you as long as you live."

The young princess, you may be sure, was not long in giving her consent; and as they spoke a magnificent coach drove up, drawn by eight beautiful horses, decked with plumes of feathers and golden harness; and behind the coach rode the prince's servant, faithful Heinrich, who had bewailed the misfortunes of his dear master during his enchantment so long and so bitterly that his heart had well-nigh burst.

They then took leave of the king, and got into the coach, and all set out, full of joy and merriment, for the prince's kingdom, which they reached safely; and there they lived happily a great many years.

*When he had clambered down the wall, he was terribly afraid,*
*for he saw the enchantress standing before him.*

# RAPUNZEL

There were once a man and a woman who had long in vain wished for a child. At length it seemed that God was about to grant their desire.

These people had a little window at the back of their house from which a splendid garden could be seen, which was full of the most beautiful flowers and herbs. It was, however, surrounded by a high wall, and no one dared to go into it because it belonged to an enchantress who had great power and was dreaded by all the world. One day the woman was standing by this window and looking down into the garden, when she saw a bed which was planted with the most beautiful rampion (sometimes called rapunzium), and it looked so fresh and green that she longed for it; she quite pined away, and began to look pale and miserable.

Then her husband was alarmed, and asked: "What ails you, dear wife?"

"Ah," she replied, "if I can't eat some of the rampion which is in the garden behind our house, I shall die."

The man, who loved her, thought: "Sooner than let your wife die, bring her some of the rampion yourself, let it cost what it will."

At twilight, he clambered down over the wall into the garden of the enchantress, hastily clutched a handful of rampion, and took it to his wife. She at once made herself a salad of it, and ate it greedily. It tasted so good to her—so very good—that the next day she longed for it three times as much as before. If he was to have any rest, her husband must once more descend into the garden. In the gloom of evening therefore, he let himself down again; but when he had clambered down the wall he was terribly afraid, for he saw the enchantress standing before him.

"How can you dare," said she, fixing him with an angry look, "descend into my garden and steal my rampion like a thief? You shall suffer for it!"

"Ah," answered he, "let mercy take the place of justice. I only made up my mind to do it out of necessity. My wife saw your rampion from the window, and felt such a longing for it that she would have died if she had not got some to eat."

Then the enchantress allowed her anger to be softened, and said to him: "If the case be as you say, I will allow you to take away with you as much rampion as you will, only I make one condition: you must give me the child which your wife will bring into the world; it shall be well treated, and I will care for it like a mother."

The man in his terror consented to everything, and when the woman was brought to bed, the enchantress appeared at once, gave the child the name of Rapunzel, and took it away with her.

Rapunzel grew into the most beautiful child under the sun. When she was twelve years old, the enchantress shut her into a tower, which lay in a forest. It had neither stairs nor door, but quite at the top was a little window. When the enchantress wanted to go in, she placed herself beneath it and cried: "Rapunzel, Rapunzel, let down your hair to me."

Rapunzel had magnificent long hair, fine as spun gold, and when she heard the voice of the enchantress she unfastened her braided tresses, wound them round one of the hooks of the window above, and let the hair fall twenty meters down, whereupon the enchantress climbed up by it.

After a year or two, it came to pass that the king's son rode through the forest and passed by the tower. Coming from it he heard a song, which was so charming that he stood still and listened. This was Rapunzel, who in her solitude passed her time in letting her sweet

*"Rapunzel, Rapunzel, let down your hair to me."*

voice resound. The king's son wanted to climb up to her, and looked for the door of the tower, but none was to be found. He rode home, but the singing had so deeply touched his heart that every day he went out into the forest and listened to it. Once, when he was thus standing behind a tree, he saw that an enchantress came there, and he heard how she cried: "Rapunzel, Rapunzel, let down your hair to me." Then Rapunzel let down the braids of her hair, and the enchantress climbed up to her.

"If that is the ladder by which one mounts, I too will try my fortune," said he, and the next day when it began to grow dark, he went to the tower and cried: "Rapunzel, Rapunzel, let down your hair to me." Immediately the hair fell down and the king's son climbed up.

At first Rapunzel was terribly frightened when a man, such as her eyes had never yet beheld, came to her; but the king's son began to talk to her quite like a friend, and told her that his heart had been so stirred that it had let him have no rest, and he had been determined to see her.

Then Rapunzel lost her fear, and when he asked her if she would take him for her husband, and she saw that he was young and handsome, she did not hesitate; she thought: "He will love me more than old Dame Gothel does"; and she said yes, and laid her hand in his. She said: "I will willingly go away with you, but I do not know how to get down. Bring with you a skein of silk every time that you come, and I will weave a ladder with it, and when that is ready I will descend, and you will take me away on your horse." They agreed that until that time he should come to her every evening, for the old woman came by day.

The enchantress remarked nothing of this, until one day Rapunzel thoughtlessly said to her: "Tell me, Dame Gothel, how it happens that you are so much heavier for me to draw up than the king's young son—he is with me in a moment."

"Ah! you wicked child," cried the enchantress. "What do I hear you say! I thought I had separated you from all the world, and yet you have deceived me!"

In her anger she clutched Rapunzel's beautiful tresses, wrapped them twice round her left hand, seized a pair of scissors with the right, and snip, snap, they were cut off, and the lovely braids lay on the ground. And she was so pitiless that she banished poor Rapunzel to a desert where she had to live in great grief and misery.

On the same day that she cast out Rapunzel, however, the enchantress fastened the braids of hair which she had cut off to the hook of the window, and when the king's son came and cried: "Rapunzel, Rapunzel, let down your hair to me," she let the hair down.

The king's son ascended, but instead of finding his dearest Rapunzel, he found the enchantress, who gazed at him with wicked and venomous looks.

"Aha!" she cried mockingly, "you would fetch your dearest, but the beautiful bird sits no longer singing in the nest; the cat has got it, and will scratch out your eyes as well. Rapunzel is lost to you; you will never see her again."

The king's son was beside himself with pain, and in his despair he leapt down from the tower. He escaped with his life, but the thorns into which he fell pierced his eyes. Then he wandered quite blind about the forest, ate nothing but roots and berries, and did naught but lament and weep over the loss of his dearest wife. Thus he roamed about in misery for some years, and at length came to the desert where Rapunzel, with the twins to which she had given birth, a boy and a girl, lived in wretchedness.

He heard a voice, and it seemed so familiar to him that he went towards it, and when he approached, Rapunzel knew him and fell on his neck and wept. Two of her tears wetted his eyes and they grew clear again, and he could see with them as before. He led her to his kingdom where they were joyfully received, and they lived for a long time afterwards, happy and contented.

# MOTHER HOLLE

Once upon a time there was a widow who had two daughters; one of them was beautiful and industrious, the other ugly and lazy. The mother, however, loved the ugly and lazy one best, because she was her own daughter, and so the other, who was only her stepdaughter, was made to do all the work of the house, and was quite the Cinderella of the family. Her stepmother sent her out every day to sit by the well in the high road, there to spin until she made her fingers bleed. Now it chanced one day that some blood fell onto the spindle, and as the girl stooped over the well to wash it off, the spindle suddenly sprang out of her hand and fell into the well. She ran home, crying, to tell of her misfortune, but her stepmother spoke harshly to her, and after giving her a violent scolding, said unkindly, "As you have let the spindle fall into the well, you may go yourself and fetch it out."

The girl went back to the well not knowing what to do, and at last in her distress she jumped into the water after the spindle.

She remembered nothing more until she awoke and found herself in a beautiful meadow, full of sunshine, and with countless flowers blooming in every direction.

She walked over the meadow, and presently she came upon a baker's oven full of bread, and the loaves cried out to her, "Take us out, take us out, or alas! we shall be burnt to a cinder; we were baked through long ago." So she took the bread-shovel and drew them all out.

She went on a little farther, till she came to a tree full of apples. "Shake me, shake me, I pray," cried the tree; "my apples, one and all, are ripe." So she shook the tree, and the apples came falling down upon her like rain; but she continued shaking until there was not a single apple left upon it. Then she carefully gathered the apples together in a heap and walked on again.

The next thing she came to was a little house, and there she saw an old woman looking out. She had such large teeth that the girl was terrified, and turned to run away. But the old woman called after her, "What are you afraid of, dear child? Stay with me; if you will do the work of my house properly for me, I will make you very happy. You must be very careful, however, to make my bed in the right way, for I wish you always to shake it thoroughly, so that the feathers fly about; then they say, down there in the world, that it is snowing; for I am Mother Holle." The old woman spoke so kindly, that the girl summoned up courage and agreed to enter into her service.

She took care to do everything according to the old woman's bidding, and every time she made the bed she shook it with all her might, so that the feathers flew about like so many snowflakes. The old woman was as good as her word: she never spoke angrily to her, and gave her roast and boiled meats every day.

So she stayed on with Mother Holle for some time, but then she began to grow unhappy. She could not at first tell why she felt sad, but she became conscious at last of great longing to go home; then she knew she was homesick, although she was a thousand times better off with Mother Holle than with her mother and sister. After waiting awhile, she went to Mother Holle and said, "I am so homesick that I cannot stay with you any longer, for although I am so happy here, I must return to my own people."

Then Mother Holle said, "I am pleased that you should want to go back to your own people, and as you have served me so well and faithfully, I will take you home myself."

Thereupon she led the girl by the hand up to a broad gateway. The gate was opened, and as the girl passed through, a shower of gold fell upon her, and the gold clung to her, so that she was covered with it from head to foot.

"That is a reward for your industry," said Mother Holle, and as she spoke she handed her the spindle which she had dropped into the well.

The gate was then closed, and the girl found herself back in the old world close to her stepmother's house. As she entered the courtyard, the cock who was perched on the well called out: "Cock-a-doodle-doo! Your golden daughter's come back to you."

Then she went in to her mother and sister, and as she was so richly covered with gold, they gave her a warm welcome. She related to them all that had happened, and when the mother heard how she had come by her great riches, she thought she should like her ugly, lazy daughter to go and try her fortune. So she made the sister go and sit by the well and spin; and the girl thrust her hand into a thorn bush and pricked her finger, so that she might drop some blood onto the spindle; then she threw it into the well and jumped in herself.

Like her sister she awoke in the beautiful meadow, and walked over it till she came to the oven. "Take us out, take us out, or alas! we shall be burnt to a cinder; we were baked through long ago," cried the loaves as before.

But the lazy girl answered, "Do you think I am going to dirty my hands for you?" and walked on.

Presently she came to the apple tree. "Shake me, shake me, I pray; my apples, one and all, are ripe," it cried.

But she only answered, "A nice thing to ask me to do, one of the apples might fall on my head," and she passed on.

At last she came to Mother Holle's house, and as she had heard all about the large teeth from her sister, she was not afraid of them, and engaged herself without delay to the old woman.

The first day she was very obedient and industrious, and exerted herself to please Mother Holle, for she thought of the gold she should get in return. The next day, however, she began to dawdle over her work, and the third day she was more idle still; then she began to lie in bed in the mornings and refused to get up. Worse still, she neglected to make the old woman's bed properly, and forgot to shake it so that the feathers might fly about. So Mother Holle very soon got tired of her, and told her she might go.

The lazy girl was delighted at this, and thought to herself, "The gold will soon be mine." Mother Holle led her, as she had led her sister, to the broad gateway; but as she was passing through, instead of the shower of gold, a great bucketful of pitch came pouring over her.

"That is in return for your services," said the old woman, and she shut the gate.

So the lazy girl had to go home covered with pitch, and the cock on the well called out: "Cock-a-doodle-doo! Your dirty daughter's come back to you."

And, try as she would, she could not get the pitch off and it stuck to her as long as she lived.

# THE VALIANT LITTLE TAILOR

One summer's morning a little tailor was sitting on his table by the window; he was in good spirits, and sewed with all his might. Then came a peasant woman down the street crying: "Good jams, cheap! Good jams, cheap!"

This rang pleasantly in the tailor's ears; he stretched his delicate head out of the window, and called: "Come up here, dear woman; here you will get rid of your goods."

The woman came up the three steps to the tailor with her heavy basket, and he made her unpack all the pots for him.

He inspected each one, lifted it up, put his nose to it, and at length said: "The jam seems to me to be good, so weigh me out four ounces, dear woman, and if it is a quarter of a pound that is of no consequence."

The woman, who had hoped to find a good sale, gave him what he desired, but went away quite angry and grumbling.

"Now, this jam shall be blessed by God," cried the little tailor, "and give me health and strength"; so he brought the bread out of the cupboard, cut himself a piece right across the loaf, and spread the jam over it.

"This won't taste bitter," said he, "but I will just finish the jacket before I take a bite."

He laid the bread near him and sewed on, in his joy making bigger and bigger stitches. In the meantime the smell of the sweet jam rose to where the flies were sitting in great numbers, and they were attracted and descended on it in hosts.

"Hi! Who invited you?" said the little tailor, and drove the unbidden guests away.

The flies, however, who understood not a word, would not be turned away, but came back again in ever-increasing companies. The little tailor at last lost all patience, and drew a piece of cloth from the hole under his worktable, and, saying: "Wait, and I will give it to you," struck it mercilessly on them.

When he drew it away and counted, there lay before him no fewer than seven, dead and with legs stretched out.

"Are you a fellow of that sort?" said he, and could not help admiring his own bravery. "The whole town shall know of this!" And the little tailor hastened to cut himself a girdle, stitched it, and embroidered on it in large letters: "Seven at one stroke."

"Why stop at the town?" he continued. "The whole world shall hear of it!" and his heart wagged with joy like a lamb's tail.

The tailor put on the girdle, and resolved to go forth into the world, because he thought his workshop was too small for his valor. Before he went away, he sought about in the house to see if there was anything which he could take with him; however, he found nothing but an old cheese, and that he put in his pocket. In front of the door he observed a bird which had caught itself in the thicket. It had to go into his pocket with the cheese. Now he took to the road boldly, and as he was light and nimble, he felt no fatigue. The road led him up a mountain, and when he had reached the highest point of it, there sat a powerful giant looking peacefully about him.

The little tailor went bravely up, spoke to him, and said: "Good day, comrade, so you are sitting there overlooking the widespread world! I am just on my way thither, and want to try my luck. Have you any inclination to go with me?"

The giant looked contemptuously at the tailor, and said: "You ragamuffin! You miserable creature!"

"Oh, indeed?" answered the little tailor and, unbuttoning his coat, showed the giant the girdle. "There may you read what kind of a man I am!"

The giant read: "Seven at one stroke," and thought that they had been men whom the tailor had killed, and began to feel a little respect for the tiny fellow. Nevertheless, he wished to try him first, and took a stone in his hand and squeezed it together so that water dropped out of it. "Do that likewise," said the giant, "if you have strength."

"Is that all?" said the tailor; "that is child's play with us!" and put his hand into his pocket, brought out the soft cheese, and pressed it until the liquid ran out of it. "Faith," said he, "that was a little better, wasn't it?"

The giant did not know what to say, and could not believe it of the little man. Then the giant picked up a stone and threw it so high that the eye could scarcely follow it. "Now, little mite of a man, do that likewise."

"Well thrown," said the tailor; "but after all the stone came down to earth again; I will throw you one which shall never come back at all," and he put his hand into his pocket, took out the bird, and threw it into the air. The bird, delighted with its liberty, rose, flew away, and did not come back.

*The tailor put his hand into his pocket, brought out the soft cheese,*
*and pressed it until the liquid ran out of it.*

"How does that shot please you, comrade?" asked the tailor.

"You can certainly throw," said the giant; "but now we will see if you are able to carry anything properly."

He took the little tailor to a mighty oak tree which lay there felled on the ground, and said: "If you are strong enough, help me to carry the tree out of the forest."

"Readily," answered the little man; "take you the trunk on your shoulders, and I will raise up the branches and twigs; after all, they are the heaviest." The giant took the trunk on his shoulder, but the tailor seated himself on a branch, and the giant, who could not look round, had to carry away the whole tree, and the little tailor into the bargain; he, behind, was quite merry and happy, and whistled the song "Three tailors rode forth from the gate," as if carrying the tree were child's play.

The giant, after he had dragged the heavy burden part of the way, could go no farther, and cried: "Hark you, I shall have to let the tree fall!"

The tailor sprang nimbly down, seized the tree with both arms as if he had been carrying it, and said to the giant: "You are such a great fellow, and yet cannot even carry the tree!"

They went on together, and as they passed a cherry tree, the giant laid hold of the top of the tree where the ripest fruit was hanging, bent it down, gave it into the tailor's hand, and bade him eat. But the little tailor was much too weak to hold the tree, and when the giant let it go, it sprang back again, and the tailor was tossed into the air with it.

When he had fallen down again without injury, the giant said: "What is this? Have you not strength enough to hold a weak twig?"

"There is no lack of strength," answered the little tailor. "Do you think that could be anything to a man who has struck down seven at one blow? I leapt over the tree because the huntsmen are shooting down there in the thicket. Jump, as I did, if you can do it."

The giant made the attempt but he could not get over the tree, and remained hanging in the branches, so that in this also the tailor kept the upper hand.

The giant said: "If you are such a valiant fellow, come with me into our cavern and spend the night with us."

The little tailor was willing, and followed him. When they went into the cave, other giants were sitting there by the fire, and each of them had a roasted sheep in his hand and was eating it. The little tailor looked round and thought: "It is much more spacious here than in my workshop." The giant showed him a bed, and said he was to lie down in it and sleep. The bed, however, was too big for the little tailor; he did not lie down in it, but crept into a corner.

When it was midnight, and the giant thought that the little tailor was lying in a sound sleep, he got up, took a great iron bar, cut through the bed with one blow, and thought he had finished off the grasshopper for good.

With the earliest dawn the giants went into the forest, and had quite forgotten the little tailor, when all at once he walked up to them quite merrily and boldly. The giants were terrified, they were afraid that he would strike them all dead, and ran away in a great hurry.

The little tailor went onwards, always following his own pointed nose. After he had walked for a long time, he came to the courtyard of a royal palace, and as he felt weary, he lay down on the grass and fell asleep.

While he lay there, the people came and inspected him on all sides, and read on his girdle: "Seven at one stroke."

"Ah!" said they, "what does the great warrior want here in the midst of peace? He must be a mighty lord." They went and announced him to the king, and gave it as their opinion that if war should break out, this would be a weighty and useful man who ought on no account to be allowed to depart. The counsel pleased the king, and he sent one of his courtiers to the little tailor to offer him military service when he awoke. The ambassador remained standing by the sleeper, waited until he stretched his limbs and opened his eyes, and then conveyed to him this proposal.

"For this very reason have I come here," the tailor replied. "I am ready to enter the king's service."

He was therefore honorably received, and a special dwelling was assigned him.

The soldiers, however, were set against the little tailor, and wished him a thousand miles away. "What is to be the end of this?" they said among themselves. "If we quarrel with him, and he strikes about him, seven of us will fall at every blow; not one of us can stand against him."

They came therefore to a decision, betook themselves in a body to the king, and begged for their dismissal. "We are not prepared," said they, "to stay with a man who kills seven at one stroke."

The king was sorry that for the sake of one he should lose all his faithful servants, wished that he had never set eyes on the tailor, and would willingly have been rid of him again. But he did not venture to give him his dismissal, for he dreaded lest he should strike him and all his people dead and place himself on the royal throne. He thought about it for a long time, and at last found good counsel. He sent to the little tailor and caused him to be informed that, as he was a great warrior, he had one request to make to him.

In a forest of his country lived two giants, who caused great mischief with their robbing, murdering, ravaging, and burning, and no one could approach them without putting himself in danger of death. If the tailor conquered and killed these two giants, he would give him his only daughter to wife, and half of his kingdom as a dowry, likewise one hundred horsemen should go with him to assist him. "That would indeed be a fine thing for a man like me!" thought the little tailor. "One is not offered a beautiful princess and half a kingdom every day of one's life!"

"Oh, yes," he replied, "I will soon subdue the giants, and do not require the help of the hundred horsemen to do it; he who can hit seven with one blow has no need to be afraid of two."

The little tailor went forth, and the hundred horsemen followed him.

When he came to the outskirts of the forest, he said to his followers: "Just stay waiting here, I alone will soon finish off the giants." Then he bounded into the forest and looked about right and left.

After a while he perceived both giants. They lay sleeping under a tree, and snored so that the branches waved up and down. The little tailor, not idle, gathered two pocketfuls of stones, and with these climbed up the tree. When he was halfway up, he slipped down by a branch until he sat just above the sleepers, and then let one stone after another fall on the breast of one of the giants. For a long time the giant felt nothing, but at last he awoke, pushed his comrade, and said: "Why are you knocking me?"

"You must be dreaming," said the other. "I am not knocking you."

They laid themselves down to sleep again, and then the tailor threw a stone down onto the second. "What is the meaning of this?" cried the other. "Why are you pelting me?"

"I am not pelting you," answered the first, growling. They disputed about it for a time, but as they were weary they let the matter rest, and their eyes closed once more.

The little tailor began his game again, picked out the biggest stone, and threw it with all his might on the breast of the first giant.

"That is too bad!" cried he, and springing up like a madman, he pushed his companion against the tree until it shook. The other paid him back in the same coin, and they got into such a rage that they tore up trees and belabored each other so long that at last they both fell down dead on the ground at the same time.

Then the little tailor leapt down. "It is a lucky thing," said he, "that they did not tear up the tree on which I was sitting, or I should have had to sprint onto another like a squirrel; but we tailors are nimble."

He drew out his sword and gave each of them a couple of thrusts in the breast, and then went out to the horsemen and said: "The work is done; I have finished both of them off, but it was hard work! They tore up trees in their sore need, and defended themselves with them, but

*They got into such a rage that they tore up trees.*

all that is to no purpose against a man like myself, who can kill seven at one blow."

"But are you not wounded?" asked the horsemen.

"You need not concern yourself about that," answered the tailor, "they have not bent one hair of mine."

The horsemen would not believe him, and rode into the forest; there they found the giants swimming in their blood, and all round about lay the torn-up trees.

The little tailor demanded of the king the promised reward; he, however, repented of his promise, and again bethought himself how he could get rid of the hero. "Before you receive my daughter, and half of my kingdom," said he, "you must perform one more heroic deed. In the forest roams a unicorn which does great harm, and you must catch it first."

"I fear one unicorn still less than two giants. Seven at one blow is my kind of affair."

He took a rope and an axe with him, went forth into the forest, and again bade those who were sent with him to wait outside. He had not long to seek. The unicorn soon came towards him, and rushed directly on the tailor, as if it would gore him with its horn without more ado. "Softly, softly; it can't be done as quickly as that," said he, and stood still and waited until the animal was quite close, and then sprang nimbly behind the tree.

The unicorn ran against the tree with all its force and stuck its horn so fast in the trunk that it had not strength enough to draw it out again, and thus it was caught. "Now, I have got the bird," said the tailor, and came out from behind the tree and put the rope round its neck, and then with his axe he hewed the horn out of the tree, and when all was ready he led the beast away and took it to the king.

The king still would not give him the promised reward, and made a third demand. Before the wedding the tailor was to catch him a wild boar that made great havoc in the forest, and the huntsmen should give him their help.

"Willingly," said the tailor, "that is child's play!" He did not take the huntsmen with him into the forest, and they were well pleased that he did not, for the wild boar had several times received them in such a manner that they had no inclination to lie in wait for him.

When the boar perceived the tailor, it ran on him with foaming mouth and whetted tusks, and was about to throw him to the ground, but the hero fled into a chapel which was near and in one bound sprang out again by the window. The boar ran after him, but the tailor ran round outside and shut the door behind it, and then the raging beast, which was much too heavy and awkward to leap out of the window, was caught.

The little tailor called the huntsmen thither that they might see the prisoner with their own eyes. The hero, however, went to the king, who was now, whether he liked it or not, obliged to keep his promise and give him his daughter and half his kingdom. Had he known that it was no warlike hero but a little tailor who was standing before him, it would have grieved him still more than it did. The wedding was held with great magnificence and small joy, and out of a tailor a king was made.

After some time the young queen heard her husband say in his dreams at night: "Boy, make me the doublet, and patch the pantaloons, or else I will rap the yard-measure over your ears." Then she discovered in what state of life the young lord had been born, and next morning complained of her wrongs to her father, and begged him to help her to get rid of her husband, who was nothing else but a tailor.

The king comforted her and said: "Leave your bedroom door open this night, and my servants shall stand outside, and when he has fallen asleep shall go in, bind him, and take him on board a ship which shall carry him into the wide world." The woman was satisfied with this; but the king's armor-bearer, who had heard all, was friendly with the young lord, and informed him of the whole plot. "I'll put a screw into that business," said the little tailor.

At night he went to bed with his wife at the usual time, and when she thought that he had fallen asleep, she got up, opened the door, and then lay down again. The little tailor, who was only pretending to be asleep, began to cry out in a clear voice: "Boy, make me the doublet and patch me the pantaloons, or I will rap the yard-measure over your ears. I smote seven at one blow. I killed two giants, I brought away one unicorn and caught a wild boar, and am I to fear those who are standing outside the room?"

When these men heard the tailor speaking thus, they were overcome by a great dread, and ran as if the wild huntsman were behind them, and none of them would venture anything further against him. So the little tailor was and remained a king to the end of his life.

# HANSEL AND GRETEL

H ard by a great forest dwelt a poor woodcutter with his wife and the two children of his former marriage. The boy was called Hansel and the girl Gretel. He earned very little, and once when a great famine fell on the land, he could no longer procure even daily bread. Now, when he thought over this by night in his bed, and tossed about in his anxiety, he groaned and said to his wife: "What is to become of us? How are we to feed our poor children when we no longer have anything even for ourselves?"

"I'll tell you what, husband," answered the woman, "early tomorrow morning we will take the children out into the forest to where it is the thickest; there we will light a fire for them, and give each of them one last piece of bread, and then we will go to our work and leave them alone. They will not find the way home again, and we shall be rid of them."

"No, wife," said the man, "I will not do that; how can I bear to leave my children alone in the forest? The wild animals would soon come and tear them to pieces."

"Oh, you fool!" said she; "then we must all four die of hunger; you may as well plane the planks for our coffins," and she left him no peace until he consented.

"But I feel very sorry for the poor children, all the same," said the man.

The two children had also not been able to sleep for hunger and had heard what their stepmother had said to their father. Gretel wept bitter tears, and said to Hansel: "Now all is over with us."

"Be quiet, Gretel," said Hansel, "do not distress yourself, I will soon find a way to help us." And when the old folk had fallen asleep, he got up, put on his little coat, opened the door below, and crept outside.

The moon shone brightly, and the white pebbles which lay in front of the house glittered like real silver pennies. Hansel stooped and stuffed the little pocket of his coat with as many as he could get in.

Then he went back and said to Gretel: "Be comforted, dear little sister, and sleep in peace, God will not forsake us," and he lay down again in his bed.

When day dawned, but before the sun had risen, the woman came and awoke the two children, saying: "Get up, you sluggards! We are going into the forest to fetch wood." She gave each a little piece of bread, and said: "There is something for your dinner, but do not eat it up before then, for you will get nothing else."

Gretel took the bread under her apron, as Hansel had the pebbles in his pocket. Then they all set out together on the way to the forest. When they had walked a short time, Hansel stood still and peeped back at the house, and did so again and again. His father said: "Hansel, what are you looking at there and staying behind for? Pay attention, and do not forget how to use your legs."

"Ah, father," said Hansel, "I am looking at my little white cat; she is sitting up on the roof, and wants to say goodbye to me."

The wife said: "Fool, that is not your little cat, that is the morning sun which is shining on the chimneys."

Hansel, however, had not been looking back at the cat, but had been constantly throwing one of the white pebble-stones out of his pocket on the road.

When they had reached the middle of the forest, the father said: "Now, children, pile up some wood, and I will light a fire that you may not be cold."

Hansel and Gretel gathered brushwood together, as high as a little hill. The brushwood was lighted, and when the flames were burning very high, the woman said: "Now, children, lay yourselves down by the fire and rest; we will go into the forest and cut some wood. When we have done, we will come back and fetch you away."

Hansel and Gretel sat by the fire, and when noon came, each ate a little piece of bread, and as they heard the strokes of the wood-axe they believed that their father was near. It was not the axe, however, but a branch which he had fastened to a withered tree which the wind was blowing backwards and forwards. And as they had been sitting such a long time, their eyes closed with fatigue, and they fell fast asleep. When at last they awoke, it was already dark night.

Gretel began to cry and said: "How are we to get out of the forest now?"

But Hansel comforted her and said: "Just wait a little, until the moon has risen, and then we will soon find the way."

And when the full moon had risen, Hansel took his little sister by the hand, and followed the pebbles which shone like newly coined silver pieces, and showed them the way.

They walked the whole night long, and by break of day came once more to their father's house. They knocked at the door, and when the woman opened it and saw that it was Hansel and Gretel, she said: "You naughty children, why have you slept so long in the forest? We thought you were never coming back at all!"

The father, however, rejoiced, for it had cut him to the heart to leave them behind alone.

Not long afterwards, there was once more great dearth throughout the land, and the children heard their mother saying at night to their father: "Everything is eaten again, we have one half-loaf left, and that is the end. The children must go, we will take them farther into the wood, so that they will not find their way out again; there is no other means of saving ourselves!" The man's heart was heavy, and he thought: "It would be better for me to share the last mouthful with my children." The woman, however, would listen to nothing that he had to say, but scolded and reproached him. He who says A must say B, likewise, and as he had yielded the first time, he had to do so a second time also.

The children, however, were still awake and had heard the conversation. When the old folk were asleep, Hansel again got up, and wanted to go out and pick up pebbles as he had done before, but the woman had locked the door, and Hansel could not get out.

Nevertheless he comforted his little sister, and said: "Do not cry, Gretel, go to sleep quietly, the good God will help us."

Early in the morning came the woman, and took the children out of their beds. Their piece of bread was given to them, but it was still smaller than the time before. On the way into the forest Hansel crumbled his in his pocket, and often stood still and threw a morsel on the ground.

"Hansel, why do you stop and look round?" said the father. "Come on, do."

"I am looking back at my little pigeon which is sitting on the roof and wants to say goodbye to me," answered Hansel.

"Fool!" said the woman, "that is not your little pigeon, that is the morning sun that is shining on the chimney."

Hansel, however, little by little, threw all the crumbs on the path.

The woman led the children still deeper into the forest, where they had never in their lives been before. Then a great fire was again made, and the mother said: "Just sit there, you children, and when you are tired you may sleep a little; we are going into the forest to cut wood, and in the evening when we are done, we will come and fetch you away."

When it was noon, Gretel shared her piece of bread with Hansel, who had scattered his by the way. Then they fell asleep and evening passed, but no one came to the poor children. They did not awake until it was dark night, and Hansel comforted his little sister and said: "Just wait, Gretel, until the moon rises, and then we shall see the crumbs of bread which I have strewn about; they will show us our way home again."

When the moon came they set out, but they found no crumbs, for the many thousands of birds which fly about in the woods and fields had picked them all up. Hansel said to Gretel: "We shall soon find the way," but they did not find it. They walked the whole night and all the next day too, from morning till evening, but they did not get out of

*A woman as old as the hills came hobbling out.*

the forest, and they were very hungry for they had had nothing to eat but two or three berries which grew on the ground. And as they were so weary that their legs would carry them no longer, they lay down beneath a tree and fell asleep.

It was now three mornings since they had left their father's house. They began to walk again, but they always came deeper into the forest, and if help did not come soon, they must die of hunger and weariness. When it was midday, they saw a beautiful snow-white bird sitting on a bough, which sang so delightfully that they stood still and listened to it. And when its song was over, it spread its wings and flew away before them, and they followed it until they reached a little house, on the roof of which it alighted; and when they approached the little house they saw that it was built of bread and covered with cakes, but that the windows were of clear sugar. "We will set to work on that," said Hansel, "and have a good meal. I will eat a bit of the roof, and you, Gretel, can eat some of the window, it will taste sweet." Hansel reached up and broke off a little of the roof to try how it tasted, and Gretel leant against the window and nibbled at the panes. Then a soft voice cried from the parlor: "Nibble, nibble, gnaw. Who is nibbling at my little house?"

The children answered: "The wind, the wind, the heaven-born wind," and went on eating without disturbing themselves. Hansel, who liked the taste of the roof, tore down a great piece of it, and Gretel pushed out the whole of one round windowpane and sat down on the ground to enjoy it.

Suddenly the door opened, and a woman as old as the hills, who supported herself on crutches, came hobbling out. Hansel and Gretel were so terribly frightened that they let fall what they had in their hands. The old woman, however, nodded her head, and said: "Oh, you dear children, who has brought you here? Do come in, and stay with me. No harm shall happen to you."

She took them both by the hand, and led them into her little house.

Then good food was set before them, milk and pancakes, with sugar, apples, and nuts. Afterwards two pretty little beds were covered with clean white linen, and Hansel and Gretel lay down in them, and thought they were in heaven.

The old woman had only pretended to be so kind; she was in reality a wicked witch, who lay in wait for children, and had only built the little house of bread in order to entice them there. When a child fell into her power, she killed it, cooked and ate it, and that was a feast day with her. Witches have red eyes, and cannot see far, but they have a keen sense of smell like the beasts, and are aware when human beings draw near. When Hansel and Gretel came into her neighborhood, she laughed with malice, and said mockingly: "I have them, they shall not escape me!"

Early in the morning before the children were awake, she was already up, and when she saw both of them sleeping and looking so pretty, with their plump and rosy cheeks, she muttered to herself: "That will be a dainty mouthful!" Then she seized Hansel with her shriveled hand, carried him into a little stable, and locked him in behind a grated door. Scream as he might, it would not help him. Then she went to Gretel, shook her till she awoke, and cried: "Get up, lazy thing, fetch some water, and cook something good for your brother; he is in the stable outside, and is to be made fat. When he is fat, I will eat him." Gretel began to weep bitterly, but it was all in vain, for she was forced to do what the wicked witch commanded.

And now the best food was cooked for poor Hansel, but Gretel got nothing but crab shells. Every morning the woman crept to the little stable, and cried: "Hansel, stretch out your finger that I may feel if you will soon be fat." Hansel, however, stretched out a little bone to her, and the old woman, who had dim eyes, could not see it, and thought it was Hansel's finger, and was astonished that there was no way of fattening him.

When four weeks had gone by, and Hansel still remained thin, she

*"Hansel, stretch out your finger that I may feel if you will soon be fat."*

was seized with impatience and would not wait any longer. "Now, then, Gretel," she cried to the girl, "stir yourself, and bring some water. Let Hansel be fat or lean, tomorrow I will kill him, and cook him."

Ah, how the poor little sister did lament when she had to fetch the water, and how her tears did flow down her cheeks! "Dear God, do help us," she cried. "If the wild beasts in the forest had but devoured us, we should at any rate have died together."

"Just keep your noise to yourself," said the old woman, "it won't help you at all."

Early in the morning, Gretel had to go out and hang up the cauldron with the water, and light the fire.

"We will bake first," said the old woman, "I have already heated

the oven, and kneaded the dough." She pushed poor Gretel out to the oven, from which flames of fire were already darting. "Creep in," said the witch, "and see if it is properly heated, so that we can put the bread in."

Once Gretel was inside, she intended to shut the oven and let her bake in it, and then she would eat her, too. But Gretel saw what she had in mind, and said: "I do not know how I am to do it; how do I get in?"

"Silly goose," said the old woman. "The door is big enough; just look, I can get in myself!" and she crept up and thrust her head into the oven. Then Gretel gave her a push that drove her far into it, and shut the iron door, and fastened the bolt. Oh! Then she began to howl quite horribly, but Gretel ran away and the wicked witch was miserably burnt to death.

Gretel, however, ran like lightning to Hansel, opened his little stable, and cried: "Hansel, we are saved! The old witch is dead!" Then Hansel sprang like a bird from its cage when the door is opened. How they did rejoice and embrace each other, and dance about and kiss each other! And as they had no longer any need to fear her, they went into the witch's house, and in every corner there stood chests full of pearls and jewels. "These are far better than pebbles!" said Hansel, and thrust into his pocket whatever could be got in, and Gretel said: "I, too, will take something home with me," and filled her pinafore full. "But now we must be off," said Hansel, "that we may get out of the witch's forest."

When they had walked for two hours, they came to a great stretch of water. "We cannot cross," said Hansel, "I see no foot-plank, and no bridge."

"And there is alas no ferry," answered Gretel; "but a white duck is swimming there: if I ask her, she will help us over." Then she cried:

*"Little duck, little duck, dost thou see,*
*Hansel and Gretel are waiting for thee?*

*There's never a plank or bridge in sight,*
*Take us across on thy back so white."*

The duck came to them, and Hansel seated himself on its back, and told his sister to sit by him. "No," replied Gretel, "that will be too heavy for the little duck; she shall take us across one after the other." The good little duck did so, and when they were once safely across and had walked for a short time, the forest seemed to be more and more familiar to them, and at length they saw from afar their father's house.

Then they began to run, rushed into the parlor, and threw themselves round their father's neck. The man had not known one happy hour since he had left the children in the forest; and the woman, who had been so cruel, was dead.

Gretel emptied her pinafore so that quantities of pearls and precious stones ran about the room, and Hansel threw one handful after another out of his pocket to add to them. Then all anxiety was at an end, and they lived together in perfect happiness.

# CAT AND MOUSE IN PARTNERSHIP

A certain cat had made the acquaintance of a mouse, and had said so much to her about the great love and friendship she felt for her, that at length the mouse agreed that they should live and keep house together.

"But we must make a provision for winter, or else we shall suffer from hunger," said the cat; "and you, little mouse, cannot venture everywhere, or you will be caught in a trap someday."

The good advice was followed, and a pot of fat was bought, but they did not know where to put it. At length, after much consideration, the cat said: "I know no place where it will be better stored up than in the church, for no one dares take anything away from there. We will set it beneath the altar, and not touch it until we are really in need of it."

So the pot was placed in safety, but it was not long before the cat had a great yearning for it, and said to the mouse: "I want to tell you something, little mouse; my cousin has brought a little son into the world, and has asked me to be godmother; he is white with brown spots, and I am to hold him over the font at the christening. Let me go out today, and you look after the house by yourself."

"Yes, yes," answered the mouse, "by all means go, and if you get anything very good to eat, think of me. I should like a drop of sweet red christening wine myself."

All this, however, was untrue; the cat had no cousin, and had not been

133

asked to be godmother. She went straight to the church, stole to the pot of fat, and began to lick at it until she had licked the top layer off. Then she took a walk upon the roofs of the town, looked out for opportunities, and then stretched herself in the sun, and licked her lips whenever she thought of the pot of fat. Not until it was evening did she return home.

"Well, here you are again," said the mouse, "no doubt you have had a merry day."

"All went off well," answered the cat.

"What name did they give the child?"

"Top-off!" said the cat quite coolly.

"Top-off!" cried the mouse. "That is a very odd and uncommon name—is it a usual one in your family?"

"So what if it is," said the cat, "it is no worse than Crumb-stealer, as your godchildren are called."

Before long the cat was seized by another fit of yearning. She said to the mouse: "You must do me a favor, and once more manage the house for a day alone. I am again asked to be godmother, and as the child has a white ring round its neck, I cannot refuse."

The good mouse consented, but the cat crept behind the town walls to the church, and devoured half the pot of fat. "Nothing ever seems so good as what one keeps to oneself," said she, and was quite satisfied with her day's work.

When she went home the mouse inquired: "And what was the child christened?"

"Half-done," answered the cat.

"Half-done! What are you saying? I never heard the name in my life. I'll wager anything it is not in any dictionary of names!"

The cat's mouth soon began to water for some more licking. "All good things go in threes," said she. "I am asked to stand godmother again. The child is quite black; it does have white paws, but with that exception, it has not a single white hair on its whole body; this only happens once every few years; you will let me go, won't you?"

*The cat crept behind the town walls to the church.*

"Top-off! Half-done!" answered the mouse. "They are such odd names, they make me very thoughtful."

"You sit at home," said the cat, "in your dark gray fur coat and long tail, and are filled with fancies; that's because you do not go out in the daytime." During the cat's absence the mouse cleaned the house, and put it in order, but the greedy cat entirely emptied the pot of fat. "When everything is eaten up one has some peace," said she to herself, and well filled and sleek she did not return home till night.

The mouse at once asked what name had been given to the third child. "It will not please you more than the others," said the cat. "He is called All-gone."

"All-gone," cried the mouse. "That is the most suspicious name of all! I have never seen it in print. All-gone; what can that mean?" and she shook her head, curled herself up, and lay down to sleep.

From this time forth no one invited the cat to be godmother, but when the winter had come and there was no longer anything to be found outside, the mouse thought of their provision, and said: "Come, cat, we will go to our pot of fat which we have stored up for ourselves— we shall enjoy that."

"Yes," answered the cat, "you will enjoy it as much as you would enjoy sticking that dainty tongue of yours out of the window."

They set out on their way, and when they arrived the pot certainly was still in its place, but it was empty.

"Alas!" said the mouse, "now I see what has happened, now it comes to light! You are some true friend! You have devoured all when you were standing godmother. First Top-off, then Half-done, then—"

"Will you hold your tongue?" cried the cat. "One word more, and I will eat you too."

"All-gone" was already on the poor mouse's lips; scarcely had she spoken it before the cat sprang on her, seized her, and swallowed her down. Verily, that is the way of the world.

# RUMPELSTILTSKIN

B y the side of a wood, in a country a long way off, ran a fine stream of water; and upon the stream there stood a mill. The miller's house was close by, and the miller, you must know, had a very beautiful daughter. She was, moreover, very shrewd and clever; and the miller was so proud of her that he one day told the king of the land, who used to come and hunt in the wood, that his daughter could spin gold out of straw.

Now this king was very fond of money; and when he heard the miller's boast his greediness was aroused, and he sent for the girl to be brought before him. Then he led her to a chamber in his palace where there was a great heap of straw, and gave her a spinning wheel, and said, "All this must be spun into gold before morning, if you love your life." It was in vain that the poor maiden said that it was only a silly boast of her father's, and that she could do no such thing as spin straw into gold; the chamber door was locked, and she was left alone.

She had sat down in one corner of the room and begun to bewail her hard fate, when on a sudden the door opened and a droll-looking little man hobbled in and said, "Good morrow to you, my good lass; what are you weeping for?"

"Alas!" said she, "I must spin this straw into gold, and know not how."

"What will you give me," said the hobgoblin, "to do it for you?"

"My necklace," replied the maiden.

He took her at her word, and sat himself down to the wheel, and whistled and sang:

*"Round about, round about,*
*Lo and behold!*
*Reel away, reel away,*
*Straw into gold!"*

And round about the wheel went merrily, the work was quickly done, and the straw was all spun into gold.

When the king came and saw this, he was greatly astonished and pleased; but his heart grew still more greedy of gain, and he shut up the poor miller's daughter again with a fresh task. Then she knew not what to do, and sat down once more to weep; but the dwarf soon opened the door, and said, "What will you give me to do your task?"

"The ring on my finger," said she. So her little friend took the ring, and began to work at the wheel again, and whistled and sang:

*"Round about, round about,*
*Lo and behold!*
*Reel away, reel away,*
*Straw into gold!"*

till, long before morning, all was done again.

The king was greatly delighted to see all this glittering treasure; but still he had not enough: so he took the miller's daughter to a yet larger heap, and said, "All this must be spun tonight; and if it is, you shall be my queen."

As soon as she was alone the dwarf came in and said, "What will you give me to spin gold for you this third time?"

"I have nothing left," said she.

"Then say you will give me," said the little man, "the first child that you may have when you are queen."

"That may never be," thought the miller's daughter; and as she knew no other way to get her task done, she said she would do what he asked.

Round went the wheel again to the old song, and the manikin once more spun the heap into gold. The king came in the morning, and, finding all he wanted, was forced to keep his word; so he married the miller's daughter, and she really became queen.

At the birth of her first little child she was very glad, and forgot the dwarf, and what she had said. But one day he came into her room, where she was sitting playing with her baby, and put her in mind of it. Then she grieved sorely at her misfortune, and said she would give him all the wealth of the kingdom if he would let her off, but in vain; yet at last her tears softened him, and he said, "I will give you three days' grace, and if during that time you tell me my name, you shall keep your child."

Now the queen lay awake all night, thinking of all the odd names that she had ever heard; and she sent messengers all over the land to find out new ones. The next day the little man came, and she began with Timothy, Ichabod, Benjamin, Jeremiah, and all the names she could remember; but to all and each of them he said, "Madam, that is not my name."

The second day she began with all the comical names she could think of: Bandylegs, Hunchback, Crookshanks, and so on; but the little gentleman still said to every one of them, "Madam, that is not my name."

The third day one of the messengers came back, and said, "I have traveled two days without hearing of any other names; but yesterday, as I was climbing a high hill among the trees of the forest, where the fox

and the hare bid each other good night, I saw a little hut; and before the hut burnt a fire; and round about the fire a funny little dwarf was dancing upon one leg, and singing:

> 'Merrily the feast I'll make.
> Today I'll brew, tomorrow bake;
> Merrily I'll dance and sing,
> For next day will a stranger bring.
> Little does my lady dream
> Rumpelstiltskin is my name!'"

When the queen heard this she jumped for joy, and as soon as her little friend came she sat down upon her throne, and called all her court round to enjoy the fun; and the nurse stood by her side with the baby in her arms, as if it was quite ready to be given up. Then the little man began to chuckle at the thought of having the poor child to take home with him to his hut in the woods; and he cried out, "Now, lady, what is my name?"

"Is it John?" asked she.

"No, madam!"

"Is it Tom?"

"No, madam!"

"Is it Jemmy?"

"It is not."

"Can your name be Rumpelstiltskin?" asked the lady slyly.

"Some witch told you that—some witch told you that!" cried the little man, and dashed his right foot in a rage so deep into the floor that he was forced to lay hold of it with both hands to pull it out.

Then he made off as best he could, while the nurse laughed and the baby crowed; and all the court jeered at him for having had so much trouble for nothing, and said, "We wish you a very good morning, and a merry feast, Mr. Rumpelstiltskin!"

*The old grandfather at last had to sit in the corner behind the stove.*

# THE OLD MAN AND HIS GRANDSON

There was once a very old man, whose eyes had become dim, whose ears had become dull of hearing, whose knees trembled, and who when he sat at table could hardly hold the spoon and spilt the broth upon the tablecloth or let it run out of his mouth.

His son and his son's wife were disgusted at this, so the old grandfather at last had to sit in the corner behind the stove, and they gave him his food in an earthenware bowl, and not even enough of it. And he used to look towards the table with his eyes full of tears. Once, too, his trembling hands could not hold the bowl, and it fell to the ground and broke. The young wife scolded him, but he said nothing and only sighed. Then they bought him a wooden bowl, for a few pence, out of which he was obliged to eat.

They were once sitting thus when the little grandson of four years old began to gather together some bits of wood upon the ground.

"What are you doing there?" asked the father.

"I am making a little trough," answered the child, "for father and mother to eat out of when I am big."

The man and his wife looked at each other for a while, and presently began to cry. Then they took the old grandfather to the table, and henceforth always let him eat with them, and likewise said nothing if he did spill a little of anything.

# SNOW WHITE

It was the middle of winter, when the broad flakes of snow were falling around, that the queen of a country many thousand miles off sat working at her window, the frame of which was made of fine black ebony; and as she sat looking out upon the snow, she pricked her finger and three drops of blood fell upon it. Then she gazed thoughtfully upon the red drops that sprinkled the white snow, and said, "Would that my little daughter may be as white as that snow, as red as that blood, and as black as this ebony windowframe!" And so it was that the little girl really did grow up—her skin was as white as snow, her cheeks as rosy as the blood, and her hair as black as ebony; and she was called Snow White.

But this queen died; and the king soon married another wife, who became queen, and was very beautiful, but so vain that she could not bear to think that anyone could be handsomer than she was. She had a fairy looking-glass, and she would gaze upon herself in it and say:

> *"Tell me, glass, tell me true!*
> *Of all the ladies in the land,*
> *Who is fairest, tell me, who?"*

And the glass had always answered: "Thou, queen, art the fairest in all the land."

But Snow White grew more and more beautiful; and when she was seven years old she was as bright as the day, and fairer than the queen herself. Then the glass one day answered the queen, when she went to look in it as usual:

*"Thou, queen, art fair,*
*and beauteous to see,*
*But Snow White is lovelier*
*far than thee!"*

When she heard this she turned pale with rage and envy, and called to one of her servants, and said, "Take Snow White away into the wide wood, that I may never see her any more."

Then the servant led her away; but his heart melted when Snow White begged him to spare her life, and he said, "I will not hurt you, thou pretty child." So he left her by herself; and though he thought it most likely that the wild beasts would tear her in pieces, he felt as if a great weight were taken off his heart when he had made up his mind not to kill her but to leave her to her fate, with the chance of someone finding and saving her.

Then poor Snow White wandered along through the wood in great fear; and the wild beasts roared about her, but none did her any harm. In the evening she came to a cottage among the hills, and went in to rest, for her little feet would carry her no farther. Everything was spruce and neat in the cottage: on the table was spread a white cloth, and there were seven little plates, seven little loaves, and seven little glasses with wine in them; and seven knives and forks laid in order; and by the wall stood seven little beds. As she was very hungry, she picked a little piece of each loaf and drank a very little wine out of each glass; and after that she thought she would lie down and rest. So she tried all the little beds; but one was too long, and another was too short, and only the seventh suited her: so there she laid herself down and went to sleep.

By and by in came the masters of the cottage. Now they were seven little dwarfs that lived among the mountains and dug and searched for gold. They lit up their seven little lamps, and saw at once that all was not right.

The first said, "Who has been sitting on my stool?"
The second, "Who has been eating off my plate?"
The third, "Who has been picking my bread?"
The fourth, "Who has been meddling with my spoon?"
The fifth, "Who has been handling my fork?"

The sixth, "Who has been cutting with my knife?"

The seventh, "Who has been drinking my wine?"

Then the first looked round and said, "Who has been lying on my bed?" And the rest came running to him, and everyone cried out that somebody had been upon his bed. But the seventh saw Snow White, and called all his brethren to come and see her; and they cried out with wonder and astonishment and brought their lamps to look at her, and said, "Good heavens! What a lovely child she is!" And they were very glad to see her, and took care not to wake her; and the seventh dwarf slept an hour with each of the other dwarfs in turn, till the night was gone.

In the morning Snow White told them all her story; and they pitied her, and said if she would keep all things in order, and cook and wash and knit and spin for them, she might stay where she was, and they would take good care of her. Then they went out all day long to their work, seeking for gold and silver in the mountains, and Snow White was left at home; but they warned her, and said, "The queen will soon find out where you are, so take care to let no one in."

But the queen, now that she thought Snow White was dead, believed that she must be the handsomest lady in the land; and she went to her glass and said:

*"Tell me, glass, tell me true!*
*Of all the ladies in the land,*
*Who is fairest, tell me, who?"*

And the glass answered:

*"Thou, queen, art the fairest in all this land:*
*But over the hills, in the greenwood shade,*
*Where the seven dwarfs their dwelling have made,*
*There Snow White is hiding her head; and she*
*Is lovelier far, O queen! than thee."*

Then the queen was very much frightened; for she knew that the glass always spoke the truth, and was sure that the servant had betrayed her. And she could not bear to think that anyone lived who was more beautiful than she was; so she dressed herself up as an old peddler, and went her way over the hills, to the place where the dwarfs dwelt. Then she knocked at the door, and cried, "Fine wares to sell!"

Snow White looked out of the window, and said, "Good day, good woman! What have you to sell?"

"Good wares, fine wares," said she; "laces and bobbins of all colors."

"I will let the old lady in; she seems to be a very good sort of body," thought Snow White, as she ran down and unbolted the door.

"Bless me!" said the old woman, "how badly your stays are laced! Let me lace them up with one of my nice new laces."

Snow White did not dream of any mischief, so she stood before the old woman; but she set to work so nimbly and pulled the lace so tight that Snow White's breath was stopped, and she fell down as if she were dead.

"There's an end to all thy beauty," said the spiteful queen, and went away home.

In the evening the seven dwarfs came home; and how grieved they were to see their faithful Snow White stretched out upon the ground, as if quite dead. However, they lifted her up, and when they found what ailed her, they cut the lace; and in a little time she began to breathe, and very soon came back to life again. Then they said, "The old woman was the queen herself; take care next time, and let no one in when we are away."

When the queen got home, she went straight to her glass and spoke to it as before; but to her great grief it still said:

> *"Thou, queen, art the fairest in all this land.*
> *But over the hills, in the greenwood shade,*
> *Where the seven dwarfs their dwelling have made,*
> *There Snow White is hiding her head; and she*
> *Is lovelier far, O queen! than thee."*

Then the blood ran cold in her heart with spite and malice to see that Snow White still lived; and she dressed herself up again, but in quite another dress from the one she wore before, and took with her a poisoned comb. When she reached the dwarfs' cottage, she knocked at the door, and cried, "Fine wares to sell!"

But Snow White said, "I dare not let anyone in."

Then the queen said, "Only look at my beautiful combs!" and gave her the poisoned one. And it looked so pretty, that she took it up and put it into her hair to try it; but the moment it touched her head, the poison was so powerful that she fell down senseless.

"There you may lie," said the queen, and went her way.

But by good luck the dwarfs came in very early that evening; and when they saw Snow White lying on the ground, they guessed what had happened, and soon found the poisoned comb. And when they took it away she got well, and told them all that had passed; and they warned her once more not to open the door to anyone.

Meantime the queen went home to her glass, and shook with rage when she read the very same answer as before; and she said, "Snow White shall die, if it cost me my life."

So she went by herself into her chamber, and got ready a poisoned apple: the outside looked very rosy and tempting, but whoever tasted it was sure to die. Then she dressed herself up as a peasant's wife, and traveled over the hills to the dwarfs' cottage, and knocked at the door; but Snow White put her head out of the window and said, "I dare not let anyone in, for the dwarfs have told me not to."

"Do as you please," said the old woman, "but at any rate take this pretty apple; I will give it you."

"No," said Snow White, "I dare not take it."

"You silly girl!" answered the other, "what are you afraid of? Do you think it is poisoned? Come! Do you eat one part, and I will eat the other." Now the apple was made up so that one side was good while the other side was poisoned. Then Snow White was much tempted

*When the dwarfs arrived home, they found Snow White lying on the ground.*

to taste, for the apple looked so very nice; and when she saw the old woman eat, she could wait no longer. But she had scarcely put the piece into her mouth, when she fell down dead upon the ground.

"This time nothing will save thee," said the queen; and she went home to her glass, and at last it said: "Thou, queen, art the fairest of all the fair."

And then her wicked heart was glad, and as happy as such a heart could be.

When evening came, and the dwarfs arrived home, they found Snow White lying on the ground: no breath came from her lips, and they were afraid that she was quite dead. They lifted her up, and combed her hair, and washed her face with wine and water; but all was in vain, for the little girl seemed quite dead. So they laid her down upon a bier, and all seven watched and bewailed her three whole days; and then they thought they would bury her: but her cheeks were still rosy, and her face looked just as it did while she was alive; so they said, "We will never bury her in the cold ground." And they made a coffin of glass, so that they might still look at her, and wrote upon it in golden letters what her name was, and that she was a king's daughter. And the coffin was set beside the cottage among the hills, and one of the dwarfs always sat by it and watched. And the birds of the air came too, and bemoaned Snow White; and first of all came an owl, and then a raven, and at last a dove, and sat by her side.

And thus Snow White lay for a long, long time, and still only looked as though she was asleep; for she was even now as white as snow, and as red as blood, and as black as ebony.

At last a prince came and called at the dwarfs' house; and he saw Snow White, and read what was written in golden letters.

Then he offered the dwarfs money, and prayed and besought them to let him take her away; but they said, "We will not part with her for all the gold in the world."

At last, however, they had pity on him, and gave him the coffin;

but the moment he lifted it up to carry it home with him, the piece of apple fell from between her lips, and Snow White awoke, and said, "Where am I?"

And the prince said, "Thou art quite safe with me."

Then he told her all that had happened, and said, "I love you far better than all the world; so come with me to my father's palace, and you shall be my wife." And Snow White consented, and went home with the prince; and everything was got ready with great pomp and splendor for their wedding.

To the feast was asked, among the rest, Snow White's old enemy the queen; and as she was dressing herself in fine rich clothes, she looked in the glass and said:

> *"Tell me, glass, tell me true!*
> *Of all the ladies in the land,*
> *Who is fairest, tell me, who?"*

And the glass answered:

> *"Thou, lady, art loveliest here, I ween;*
> *But lovelier far is the new-made queen."*

When she heard this she started with rage; but her envy and curiosity were so great, that she could not help setting out to see the bride. And when she got there, and saw that it was no other than Snow White, who she thought had been dead a long while, she choked with rage and fell down and died; but Snow White and the prince lived and reigned happily over that land many, many years; and sometimes they went up into the mountains, and paid a visit to the little dwarfs, who had been so kind to Snow White in her time of need.

*It was now a sorry time for the poor little girl.*

# CINDERELLA

The wife of a rich man fell sick; and when she felt that her end drew nigh, she called her only daughter to her bedside, and said, "Always be a good girl, and I will look down from heaven and watch over you."

Soon afterwards she shut her eyes and died, and was buried in the garden; and the little girl went every day to her grave and wept, and was always good and kind to all about her.

And the snow fell and spread a beautiful white covering over the grave; but by the time the spring came, and the sun had melted it away again, her father had married another wife. This new wife had two daughters of her own that she brought home with her; they were fair in face but foul at heart, and it was now a sorry time for the poor little girl.

"What does the good-for-nothing want in the parlor?" said they; "they who would eat bread should first earn it; away with the kitchen maid!"

Then they took away her fine clothes, and gave her an old gray frock to put on, and laughed at her, and turned her into the kitchen. There she was forced to do hard work; to rise early before daylight, to bring the water, to make the fire, to cook, and to wash. Besides that, the sisters plagued her in all sorts of ways, and laughed at her. In the evening when she was tired, she had no bed to lie down on, but was made to lie by the hearth among the ashes; and as this, of course, made her always dusty and dirty, they called her Cinderella.

It happened one day that the father was going to the fair, and he asked his wife's daughters what he should bring them.

"Fine clothes," said the first;

"Pearls and diamonds," cried the second.

"Now, child," said he to his own daughter, "what will you have?"

"The first twig, dear father, that brushes against your hat when you turn your face to come homewards," said she.

Then he bought for the first two the fine clothes and pearls and diamonds they had asked for; and on his way home, as he rode through a green copse, a hazel twig brushed against him, and almost pushed off his hat: so he broke it off and brought it away; and when he got home he gave it to his daughter. Then she took it, and went to her mother's grave and planted it there; and cried so much that it was watered with her tears; and there it grew and became a fine tree. Three times every day she went to it and cried; and soon a little bird came and built its nest upon the tree, and talked with her, and watched over her, and brought her whatever she wished for.

Now it happened that the king of that land held a feast, which was to last three days; and out of those who came to it his son was to choose a bride for himself. Cinderella's two sisters were asked to come, so they called her up, and said, "Now, comb our hair, brush our shoes, and tie our sashes for us, for we are going to dance at the king's feast."

Then she did as she was told; but when all was done she could not help crying, for

she should so have liked to have gone with them to the ball; and at last she begged her mother very hard to let her go.

"You, Cinderella!" said she; "you who have nothing to wear, no clothes at all, and who cannot even dance—you want to go to the ball?" And when the girl kept on begging, she said at last, to get rid of her, "I will throw this dishful of peas into the ash heap, and if in two hours' time you have picked them all out, you shall go to the feast too."

Then she threw the peas down among the ashes, but the little maiden ran out at the back door into the garden, and cried out:

> *"Hither, hither, through the sky,*
> *Turtledoves and linnets, fly!*
> *Blackbird, thrush, and chaffinch gay,*
> *Hither, hither, haste away!*
> *One and all come help me, quick!*
> *Haste ye, haste ye—pick, pick, pick!"*

Then first came two white doves, flying in at the kitchen window; next came two turtledoves; and after them came all the little birds under heaven, chirping and fluttering in, and they flew down into the ashes. And the little doves stooped their heads down and set to work, pick, pick, pick; and then the others began to pick, pick, pick; and among them all they soon picked out all the peas and put them into the dish, but left the ashes. Long before the end of the hour the work was quite done, and all flew out again at the windows.

Then Cinderella brought the dish to her mother, overjoyed at the thought that now she should go to the ball. But the mother said, "No, no, you wretch! You have no clothes, and cannot dance; you shall not go." And when Cinderella begged very hard to go, she said, "If you can in one hour's time pick two of those dishes of peas out of the ashes, you shall go." And thus she thought she should at least get rid of her. So she shook two dishes of peas into the ashes.

But the little maiden went out into the garden at the back of the house, and cried out as before:

*"Hither, hither, through the sky,*
*Turtledoves and linnets, fly!*
*Blackbird, thrush, and chaffinch gay,*
*Hither, hither, haste away!*
*One and all come help me, quick!*
*Haste ye, haste ye—pick, pick, pick!"*

Then first came two white doves in at the kitchen window; next came two turtledoves; and after them came all the little birds under heaven, chirping and hopping about. And they flew down into the ashes; and the little doves put their heads down and set to work, pick, pick, pick; and then the others began to pick, pick, pick; and they put all the peas into the dishes, and left all the ashes. Before half an hour's time all was done, and out they flew again.

And then Cinderella took the dishes to her mother, rejoicing to think that she should now go to the ball. But her mother said, "It is all of no use, you cannot go; you have no clothes, and cannot dance, and you would only put us to shame"—and off she went with her two daughters to the ball.

Now when all were gone, and nobody left at home, Cinderella went sorrowfully and sat down under the hazel tree and cried out:

*"Shake, shake, hazel tree,*
*Gold and silver over me!"*

Then her friend the bird flew out of the tree, and brought a gold and silver dress for her, and slippers of spangled silk; and she put them on, and followed her sisters to the feast. But they did not know her, and thought it must be some strange princess, she looked so fine and beautiful in her rich clothes; and they never once thought of Cinderella, taking it for granted that she was safe at home in the dirt.

The king's son soon came up to her, and took her by the hand and danced with her and no one else; and never left her side, and when anyone else came to ask her to dance, he said, "This lady is dancing with me."

Thus they danced till a late hour of the night, and then she wanted to go home; and the king's son said, "I shall go and take care of you to your home"; for he wanted to see where the beautiful maiden lived. But she slipped away from him, unawares, and ran off towards home; and as the prince followed her, she jumped up into the pigeon house and shut the door. Then he waited till her father came home, and told him that the unknown maiden, who had been at the feast, had hid herself in the pigeon house. But when they had broken open the door they found no one within; and as they came back into the house, Cinderella was lying, as she always did, in her dirty frock by the ashes, and her dim little lamp was burning in the chimney. For she had run as quickly as she could through the pigeon house and onto the hazel tree, and had there taken off her beautiful clothes, and put them beneath the tree, that the bird might carry them away, and had lain down again amid the ashes in her little gray frock.

The next day when the feast was again held, and her father, mother, and sisters were gone, Cinderella went to the hazel tree and said:

> *"Shake, shake, hazel tree,*
> *Gold and silver over me!"*

And the bird came and brought a still finer dress than the one she had worn the day before. And when she came in it to the ball, everyone wondered at her beauty; and the king's son, who was waiting for her, took her by the hand, and danced with her; and when anyone asked her to dance, he said as before, "This lady is dancing with me."

*She looked so fine and beautiful in her rich clothes.*

When night came she wanted to go home, and the king's son followed her as before, that he might see into what house she went; but she sprang away from him all at once into the garden behind her father's house. In this garden stood a fine large pear tree full of ripe fruit; and Cinderella, not knowing where to hide herself, jumped up into it without being seen. Then the king's son lost sight of her, and could not find out where she was gone, but waited till her father came home, and said to him, "The unknown lady who danced with me has slipped away, and I think she must have sprung into the pear tree." The father thought to himself, "Can it be Cinderella?" So he had an axe brought; and they cut down the tree, but found no one upon it. And when they came back into the kitchen, there lay Cinderella among the ashes; for she had slipped down on the other side of the tree, and carried her beautiful clothes back to the bird at the hazel tree, and then put on her little gray frock.

The third day, when her father and mother and sisters were gone, she went again into the garden and said:

*"Shake, shake, hazel tree,*
*Gold and silver over me!"*

Then her kind friend the bird brought a dress still finer than the former one, and slippers which were all of gold, so that when she came to the feast no one knew what to say for wonder at her beauty; and the king's son danced with nobody but her; and when anyone else asked her to dance, he said, "This lady is my partner, sir."

When night came she wanted to go home; and the king's son would go with her, and said

to himself, "I will not lose her this time"; but, somehow, she again slipped away from him, though in such a hurry that she dropped her left golden slipper upon the stairs.

The prince took the shoe, and went the next day to the king his father, and said, "I will take for my wife the lady that this golden slipper fits." Then both the sisters were overjoyed to hear it; for they had beautiful feet, and had no doubt that they could wear the golden slipper. The eldest went first into the room where the slipper was, and wanted to try it on, and the mother stood by. But her great toe could not go into it, and the shoe was altogether much too small for her. Then the mother gave her a knife, and said, "Never mind, cut it off; when you are queen you will not care about toes; you will not want to walk." So the silly girl cut off her great toe, and thus squeezed on the shoe, and went to the king's son. Then he took her for his bride, and set her beside him on his horse, and rode away with her homewards.

But on their way home they had to pass by the hazel tree that Cinderella had planted; and on the branch sat a little dove singing:

*"Back again! Back again! Look to the shoe!*
*The shoe is too small, and not made for you!*
*Prince! Prince! Look again for thy bride,*
*For she's not the true one that sits by thy side."*

Then the prince got down and looked at her foot; and he saw, by the blood that streamed from it, what a trick she had played him. So he turned his horse round, and brought the false bride back to her home, and said, "This is not the right bride; let the other sister try and put on the slipper."

Then she went into the room and got her foot into the shoe, all but the heel, which was too large. But her mother squeezed it in till the blood came, and took her to the king's son, and he set her as his bride by his side on his horse, and rode away with her.

But when they came to the hazel tree the little dove sat there still, and sang:

> *"Back again! Back again! Look to the shoe!*
> *The shoe is too small, and not made for you!*
> *Prince! Prince! Look again for thy bride,*
> *For she's not the true one that sits by thy side."*

Then he looked down, and saw that the blood streamed so much from the shoe, that her white stockings were quite red. So he turned his horse and brought her also back again. "This is not the true bride," said he to the father; "have you no other daughters?"

"No," said he; "there is only a little dirty Cinderella here, the child of my first wife; I am sure she cannot be the bride." The prince told him to send her.

But the mother said, "No, no, she is much too dirty; she will not dare to show herself."

However, the prince would have her come; and she first washed her face and hands, and then went in and curtsied to him, and he reached her the golden slipper. Then she took her clumsy shoe off her left foot, and put on the golden slipper; and it fitted her as if it had been made for her. And when he drew near and looked at her face he knew her, and said, "This is the right bride."

But the mother and both the sisters were frightened, and turned pale with anger as he took Cinderella on his horse, and rode away with her. And when they came to the hazel tree, the white dove sang:

*"Home! Home! Look at the shoe!*
*Princess! The shoe was made for you!*
*Prince! Prince! Take home thy bride,*
*For she is the true one that sits by thy side!"*

And when the dove had done its song, it came flying, and perched upon her right shoulder, and so went home with her.

# THE TURNIP

There were two brothers who were both soldiers; the one was rich and the other poor. The poor man thought he would try to better himself; so, pulling off his red coat, he became a gardener, and dug his ground well, and sowed turnips.

When the seed came up, there was one plant bigger than all the rest; and it kept getting larger and larger, and seemed as if it would never cease growing, so that it might have been called the prince of turnips— for there never was such a one seen before, and never will be such a one seen again. At last it was so big that it filled a cart, and two oxen could hardly draw it; and the gardener knew not what in the world to do with it, nor whether it would be a blessing or a curse to him.

One day he said to himself, "What shall I do with it? If I sell it, it will bring no more than another; and for eating, the little turnips are better than this; the best thing perhaps is to carry it and give it to the king as a mark of respect."

Then he yoked his oxen, and drew the turnip to the court, and gave it to the king. "What a wonderful thing!" said the king. "I have seen many strange things, but such a monster as this I never saw. Where did you get the seed? Or is it only your good luck? If so, you are a true child of fortune."

"Ah, no!" answered the gardener. "I am no child of fortune; I am a poor soldier, who never could get enough to live upon; so I laid aside my red coat, and set to work, tilling the ground. I have a brother, who is rich, and your majesty knows him well, and all the world knows him;

but because I am poor, everybody forgets me."

The king then took pity on him, and said, "You shall be poor no longer. I will give you so much that you shall be even richer than your brother." Then he gave him gold and lands and flocks, and made him so rich that his brother's fortune could not at all be compared with his.

When the brother heard of all this, and how a turnip had made the gardener so rich, he envied him sorely, and bethought him how he could contrive to get the same good fortune for himself. However, he determined to manage more cleverly than his brother, and got together a rich present of gold and fine horses for the king; and thought he must have a much larger gift in return; for if his brother had received so much for only a turnip, what must his present be worth?

The king took the gift very graciously, and said he knew not what to give in return more valuable and wonderful than the great turnip; so the soldier was forced to put it into a cart, and drag it home with him. When he reached home, he knew not upon whom to vent his rage and spite; and at length wicked thoughts came into his head, and he resolved to kill his brother.

So he hired some villains to murder him; and having shown them where to lie in ambush, he went to his brother, and said, "Dear brother, I have found a hidden treasure; let us go and dig it up, and share it between us." The other had no suspicions of his roguery, so they went out together, and as they were traveling along, the murderers rushed out upon him, bound him, and were going to hang him on a tree.

But while they were getting all ready, they heard the trampling of a horse at a distance, which so frightened them that they pushed their prisoner headfirst into a sack, and swung him up by a cord to the tree, where they left him dangling, and ran away. Meantime he worked and worked away, till he made a hole large enough to put out his head.

When the horseman came up, he proved to be a student, a merry fellow, who was journeying along on his nag and singing as he went. As soon as the man in the sack saw him passing under the tree, he cried out, "Good morning! Good morning to thee, my friend!"

The student looked about everywhere; and seeing no one, and not knowing where the voice came from, cried out, "Who calls me?"

Then the man in the tree answered, "Lift up thine eyes, for behold here I sit in the sack of wisdom; here have I, in a short time, learnt great and wondrous things. Compared to this seat, all the learning of the schools is as empty air. A little longer, and I shall know all that man can know, and shall come forth wiser than the wisest of mankind. Here I discern the signs and motions of the heavens and the stars; the laws that control the winds; the number of the sands on the seashore; the healing of the sick; the virtues of all simples, of birds and of precious stones. Wert thou but once here, my friend, thou wouldst feel and own the power of knowledge."

The student listened to all this and wondered much; at last he said, "Blessed be the day and hour when I found you; cannot you contrive to let me into the sack for a little while?"

Then the other answered, as if very unwillingly, "A little space I may allow thee to sit here, if thou wilt reward me well and entreat me kindly; but thou must tarry yet an hour below, till I have learnt some little matters that are yet unknown to me."

So the student sat himself down and waited a while; but the time hung heavy upon him, and he begged earnestly that he might ascend forthwith, for his thirst for knowledge was great.

Then the other pretended to give way, and said, "Thou must let the sack of wisdom descend, by untying yonder cord, and then thou shalt enter."

So the student let him down, opened the sack, and set him free. "Now then," cried he, "let me ascend quickly."

As he began to put himself into the sack heels first, "Wait a while," said the gardener, "that is not the way."

Then he pushed him in headfirst, tied up the sack, and soon swung up the searcher after wisdom until he was dangling in the air.

"How is it with thee, friend?" said he. "Dost thou not feel that wisdom comes unto thee? Rest there in peace, till thou art a wiser man than thou wert."

So saying, he trotted off on the student's nag, and left the poor fellow to gather wisdom till somebody should come and let him down.

# THE WOLF AND THE SEVEN LITTLE KIDS

There was once upon a time an old goat who had seven little kids, and loved them with all the love of a mother for her children. One day she wanted to go into the forest and fetch some food. So she called all seven to her and said: "Dear children, I have to go into the forest; be on your guard against the wolf; if he comes in, he will devour you all—skin, hair, and everything. The wretch often disguises himself, but you will know him at once by his rough voice and his black feet."

The kids said: "Dear mother, we will take good care of ourselves; you may go away without any anxiety." Then the old one bleated, and went on her way with an easy mind.

It was not long before someone knocked at the house door and called: "Open the door, dear children; your mother is here, and has brought something back with her for each of you."

But the little kids knew that it was the wolf, by the rough voice. "We will not open the door," cried they, "you are not our mother. She has a soft, pleasant voice, but your voice is rough; you are the wolf!"

Then the wolf went away to a shopkeeper and bought himself a great lump of chalk, ate this, and made his voice soft with it. Then he came back, knocked at the door of the house, and called: "Open the door, dear children, your mother is here and has brought something back with her for each of you."

But the wolf had laid his black paws against the window, and the children saw them and cried: "We will not open the door, our mother has not black feet like you: you are the wolf!"

Then the wolf ran to a baker and said: "I have hurt my feet, rub some dough over them for me." And when the baker had rubbed his feet over, he ran to the miller and said: "Strew some white meal over my feet for me."

The miller thought to himself: "The wolf wants to deceive someone," and refused; but the wolf said: "If you will not do it, I will devour you." Then the miller was afraid, and made his paws white for him. Truly, this is the way of mankind.

So now the wretch went for the third time to the house door, knocked at it, and said: "Open the door for me, children, your dear little mother has come home, and has brought every one of you something back from the forest with her."

The little kids cried: "First show us your paws that we may know if you are our dear little mother."

Then he put his paws in through the window, and when the kids saw that they were white, they believed that all he said was true, and opened the door. But who should come in but the wolf! They were terrified and wanted to hide themselves. One sprang under the table, the second into the bed, the third into the stove, the fourth into the kitchen, the fifth into the cupboard, the sixth under the washing bowl, and the seventh into the clock case. But the wolf found them all, and used no great ceremony; one after the other he swallowed them down his throat. The youngest, who was in the clock case, was the only one he did not find.

When the wolf had satisfied his appetite he took himself off, laid himself down under a tree in the green meadow outside, and began to sleep. Soon afterwards the old goat came home again from the forest. Ah! what a sight she saw there! The house door stood wide open. The table, chairs, and benches were thrown down, the washing bowl lay broken to pieces, and the quilts and pillows were pulled off the bed. She sought her children, but they were nowhere to be found. She called them one after another by name, but no one answered. At last, when she came to the youngest, a soft voice cried: "Dear mother, I am in the clock case." She took the kid out, and it told her that the wolf had come and had eaten all the others. Then you may imagine how she wept over her poor children.

At length in her grief she went out, and the youngest kid ran with her. When they came to the meadow, there lay the wolf by the tree and snored so loud that the branches shook. She looked at him on every side and saw that something was moving and struggling in his gorged belly. "Ah, heavens," she said, "is it possible that my poor children, whom he has swallowed down for his supper, can be still alive?" Then the kid had to run home and fetch scissors and a needle and thread, and the goat cut open the monster's stomach, and hardly had she made one cut, than one little kid thrust its head out, and when she had cut farther, all six sprang out one after another, and were all still alive, and had suffered no injury whatever, for in his greediness the monster had swallowed them down whole.

What rejoicing there was! They embraced their dear mother, and jumped like a tailor at his wedding. The mother, however, said: "Now go and look for some big stones, and we will fill the wicked beast's stomach with them while he is still asleep." Then the seven kids dragged the stones thither with all speed, and put as many of them into this stomach as they could get in; and the mother sewed him up again in the greatest haste, so that he was not aware of anything and never once stirred.

When the wolf at length had had his fill of sleep, he got on his legs, and as the stones in his stomach made him very thirsty, he wanted to go to a well to drink. But when he began to walk and to move about, the stones in his stomach knocked against each other and rattled. Then cried he:

*"What rumbles and tumbles*
*Against my poor bones?*
*I thought 'twas six kids,*
*But it feels like big stones."*

And when he got to the well and stooped over the water to drink, the heavy stones made him fall in, and he drowned miserably. When the seven kids saw that, they came running to the spot and cried aloud: "The wolf is dead! The wolf is dead!" and danced for joy round about the well with their mother.

*"The wolf is dead! The wolf is dead!"*

*So the four brothers took their walking sticks in their hands, and their little bundles on their shoulders, and went all out at the gate together.*

# THE FOUR CLEVER BROTHERS

Dear children," said a poor man to his four sons, "I have nothing to give you; you must go out into the wide world and try your luck. Begin by learning some craft or another, and see how you can get on." So the four brothers took their walking sticks in their hands, and their little bundles on their shoulders, and after bidding their father goodbye, went all out at the gate together.

When they had got on some way they came to four crossways, each leading to a different country.

Then the eldest said, "Here we must part; but this day four years hence we will come back to this spot, and in the meantime each must try what he can do for himself."

So each brother went his way; and as the eldest was hastening on a man met him, and asked him where he was going, and what he wanted. "I am going to try my luck in the world, and should like to begin by learning some art or trade," answered he.

"Then," said the man, "go with me, and I will teach you to become the cunningest thief that ever was."

"No," said the other, "that is not an honest calling, and what can one look to earn by it in the end but the gallows?"

"Oh!" said the man, "you need not fear the gallows; for I will only teach you to steal what will be fair game: I meddle with nothing except what no one else wants or cares anything about, and only do it where no one can find you out."

So the young man agreed to follow his trade, and he soon showed himself so clever that nothing could escape him that he had once set his mind upon.

The second brother also met a man, who, when he found out what he was setting out upon, asked him what craft he meant to follow.

"I do not know yet," said he.

"Then come with me, and be a stargazer. It is a noble art, for nothing can be hidden from you when once you understand the stars."

The plan pleased him much, and he soon became such a skillful stargazer that, when he had served out his time, his master gave him a glass, and said, "With this you can see all that is passing in the sky and on earth, and nothing can be hidden from you."

The third brother met a huntsman, who took him with him and taught him so well all that belonged to hunting that he became very clever in the craft of the woods; and when he came to leave, his master gave him a bow, and said, "Whatever you shoot at with this bow you will be sure to hit."

The youngest brother likewise met a man who asked him what he wished to do. "Would not you like," said he, "to be a tailor?"

"Oh, no!" said the young man; "sitting cross-legged from morning to night, working backwards and forwards with a needle or an iron, will never suit me."

"Oh!" answered the man, "that is not my sort of tailoring; come with me, and you will learn quite another kind of craft from that."

Not knowing what better to do, he fell in with the plan, and learnt tailoring from the beginning; and when he left, his master gave him a needle and said, "You can sew anything with this, be it as soft as an egg or as hard as steel; and the joint will be so fine that no seam will be seen."

After the space of four years, at the time agreed upon, the four brothers met at the crossroads, and having welcomed each other, set off towards their father's home, where they told him all that had happened to them, and how each had learned some craft.

Then, one day, as they were sitting before the house under a very high tree, the father said, "I should like to try what each of you can do in this way."

So he looked up, and said to the second son, "At the top of this tree there is a chaffinch's nest; tell me how many eggs there are in it."

The stargazer took his glass, looked up, and said, "Five."

"Now," said the father to the eldest son, "take away the eggs without letting the bird that is sitting upon them and hatching them know anything of what you are doing."

So the cunning thief climbed up the tree, and brought away to his father the five eggs from under the bird; and it never saw or felt what he was doing, but kept sitting on at its ease.

Then the father took the eggs, and put one on each corner of the table, and the fifth in the middle, and said to the huntsman, "Cut all the eggs in two pieces at one shot." The huntsman took up his bow, and at one shot struck all the five eggs as his father wished.

"Now comes your turn," said he to the young tailor; "sew the eggs and the young birds in them together again, so neatly that the shot shall have done them no harm."

Then the tailor took his needle, and sewed the eggs as he was told; and when he had done, the thief was sent to take them back to the nest, and put them under the bird without its knowing it.

Then she went on sitting, and hatched them, and in a few days they crawled out, and had only a little red streak across their necks where the tailor had sewn them together.

"Well done, sons!" said the old man; "you have made good use of your time, and learnt something worth the knowing; but I am sure I do not know which ought to have the prize. Oh, that a time might soon come for you to turn your skill to some account!"

Not long after this there was a great bustle in the country; for the king's daughter had been carried off by a mighty dragon, and the king mourned over his loss day and night, and made it known that whoever brought her back to him should have her for a wife.

*The king's daughter had been carried off by a mighty dragon.*

Then the four brothers said to each other, "Here is a chance for us; let us try what we can do." And they agreed to see whether they could not set the princess free.

"I must first find out where she is, however," said the stargazer, as he looked through his glass; and he soon cried out, "I see her afar off, sitting upon a rock in the sea, and I can spy the dragon close by, guarding her."

Then he went to the king, and asked for a ship for himself and his brothers; and they sailed together over the sea, till they came to the right place. There they found the princess sitting, as the stargazer had said, on the rock; and the dragon was lying asleep, with his head upon her lap. "I dare not shoot at him," said the huntsman, "for I should kill the beautiful young lady also."

"Then I will try my skill," said the thief, and went and stole her away from under the dragon, so quietly and gently that the beast did not know it, but went on snoring.

Then away they hastened with her, full of joy, in their boat towards the ship; but soon came the dragon roaring behind them through the air; for he awoke and missed the princess. But when he got over the boat, and wanted to pounce upon them and carry off the princess, the huntsman took up his bow and shot him straight through the heart so that he fell down dead. They were still not safe; for he was such a great beast that in his fall he overset the boat, and they had to swim in the open sea, clinging to a few planks.

So the tailor took his needle, and with a few large stitches fixed some of the planks together; and he sat down upon these, and sailed about, and gathered up all the pieces of the boat; and then tacked them together so quickly that the boat was soon ready, and they then reached the ship and got home safe.

When they had brought home the princess to her father, there was great rejoicing; and he said to the four brothers, "One of you shall marry her, but you must settle among yourselves which it is to be."

Then there arose a quarrel between them; and the stargazer said, "If I had not found the princess, all your skill would have been of no use; therefore she ought to be mine."

"Your seeing her would have been of no use," said the thief, "if I had not taken her away from the dragon; therefore she ought to be mine."

"No, she is mine," said the huntsman; "for if I had not killed the dragon, he would, after all, have torn you and the princess into pieces."

"And if I had not sewn the boat together again," said the tailor, "you would all have been drowned; therefore she is mine."

Then the king put in a word, and said, "Each of you is right; and as all of you cannot have the young lady, the best way is for none of you to have her; for the truth is, there is somebody she likes a great deal better. But to make up for your loss, I will give each of you, as a reward for his skill, half a kingdom." So the brothers agreed that this plan would be much better than either quarreling or marrying a lady who had no mind to have them.

And the king then gave to each half a kingdom, as he had promised; and they lived very happily the rest of their days, and took good care of their father; and somebody took better care of the young lady than to let either the dragon or one of the craftsmen have possession of her again.

# THE WHITE SNAKE

Along time ago there lived a king who was famed for his wisdom through all the land. Nothing was hidden from him, and it seemed as if news of the most secret things was brought to him through the air. But he had a strange custom; every day after dinner, when the table was cleared, and no one else was present, a trusty servant had to bring him one more dish. It was covered, however, and even the servant did not know what was in it, neither did anyone know, for the king never took off the cover to eat of it until he was quite alone.

This had gone on for a long time, when one day the servant, who took away the dish, was overcome with such curiosity that he could not help carrying the dish into his room. When he had carefully locked the door, he lifted up the cover, and saw a white snake lying on the dish. But when he saw it he could not deny himself the pleasure of tasting it, so he cut off a little bit and put it into his mouth. No sooner had it touched his tongue than he heard a strange whispering of little voices outside his window. He went and listened, and then noticed that it was the sparrows who were chattering together, and telling one another of all kinds of things which they had seen in the fields and woods. Eating the snake had given him the power of understanding the language of animals.

Now it so happened that on this very day the queen lost her most beautiful ring, and suspicion of having stolen it fell upon this trusty servant, who was allowed to go everywhere. The king ordered the man to be brought before him, and threatened with angry words that unless he could before the morrow point out the thief, he himself should be looked upon as guilty and executed. In vain he declared his innocence; he was dismissed with no better answer.

In his trouble and fear he went down into the courtyard and took thought how to help himself out of his trouble. Now some ducks were sitting together quietly by a brook and taking their rest; and, while they were making their feathers smooth with their bills, they were having a confidential conversation together. The servant stood by and listened. They were telling one another of all the places where they had been waddling about all the morning, and what good food they had found; and one said in a pitiful tone: "Something lies heavy on my stomach; as I was eating in haste I swallowed a ring which lay under the queen's window." The servant at once seized her by the neck, carried her to the kitchen, and said to the cook: "Here is a fine duck; pray, kill her."

"Yes," said the cook, and weighed her in his hand; "she has spared no trouble to fatten herself, and has been waiting to be roasted long enough." So he cut off her head, and as she was being dressed for the spit, the queen's ring was found inside her.

The servant could now easily prove his innocence; and the king, to make amends for the wrong, allowed him to ask a favor, and promised him the best place in the court that he could wish for. The servant refused everything, and only asked for a horse and some money for traveling, as he had a mind to see the world and go about a little. When his request was granted, he set out on his way, and one day came to a pond, where he saw three fishes caught in the reeds and gasping for water. Now, though it is said that fishes are dumb, he heard them lamenting that they must perish so miserably, and, as he had a kind heart, he got off his horse and put the three prisoners back into the water. They leapt with delight, put out their heads, and cried to him: "We will remember you and repay you for saving us!"

He rode on, and after a while it seemed to him that he heard a voice in the sand at his feet. He listened, and heard an ant-king complain:

*"We will remember you and repay you for saving us!"*

"Why cannot folks, with their clumsy beasts, keep off our bodies? That stupid horse, with his heavy hoofs, has been treading down my people without mercy!" So he turned onto a side path and the ant-king cried out to him: "We will remember you—one good turn deserves another!"

The path led him into a wood, and there he saw two old ravens standing by their nest, and throwing out their young ones. "Out with you, you idle, good-for-nothing creatures!" cried they; "we cannot find food for you any longer; you are big enough, and can provide for yourselves." But the poor young ravens lay upon the ground, flapping their wings, and crying: "Oh, what helpless chicks we are! We must shift for ourselves, and yet we cannot fly! What can we do, but lie here and starve?" So the good young fellow alighted and killed his horse with his sword, and gave it to them for food. Then they came hopping up to it, satisfied their hunger, and cried: "We will remember you— one good turn deserves another!"

And now he had to use his own legs, and when he had walked a long way, he came to a large city. There was a great noise and crowd in the streets, and a man rode up on horseback, crying aloud: "The king's daughter wants a husband; but whoever seeks her hand must perform a hard task, and if he does not succeed he will forfeit his life." Many had already made the attempt, but in vain; nevertheless when the youth saw the king's daughter he was so overcome by her great beauty that he forgot all danger, went before the king, and declared himself a suitor.

So he was led out to the sea, and a gold ring was thrown into it, before his eyes; then the king ordered him to fetch this ring up from the bottom of the sea, and added: "If you come up again without it you will be thrown in again and again until you perish amid the waves." All the people grieved for the handsome youth; then they went away, leaving him alone by the sea.

He stood on the shore and considered what he should do; suddenly he saw three fishes come swimming towards him, and they were the very fishes whose lives he had saved. The one in the middle held a mussel in its mouth, which it laid on the shore at the youth's feet, and when he had taken it up and opened it, there lay the gold ring in the shell. Full of joy he took it to the king and expected that he would grant him the promised reward.

But when the proud princess perceived that he was not her equal in birth, she scorned him, and required him first to perform another task. She went down into the garden and strewed with her own hands ten sackfuls of millet seed on the grass; then she said: "Tomorrow morning before sunrise these must be picked up, and not a single grain be wanting."

The youth sat down in the garden and considered how it might be possible to perform this task, but he could think of nothing, and there he sat sorrowfully awaiting the break of day, when he should be led to his death. But as soon as the first rays of the sun shone into the garden he saw all the ten sacks standing side by side, quite full, and not a single grain was missing. The ant-king had come in the night with thousands and thousands of ants, and the grateful creatures had by great industry picked up all the millet seeds and gathered them into the sacks.

Presently the king's daughter herself came down into the garden, and was amazed to see that the young man had done the task she had given him. But she could not yet conquer her proud heart, and said: "Although he has performed both the tasks, he shall not be my husband until he has brought me the Golden Apple from the Tree of Life."

The youth did not know where the Tree of Life stood, but he set out, and would have gone on forever, as long as his legs would carry him, though he had no hope of finding it. After he had wandered through three kingdoms, he came one evening to a wood, and lay down under a tree to sleep. But he heard a rustling in the branches, and a golden apple fell into his hand. At the same time three ravens flew down to him, perched themselves upon his knee, and said: "We are the three young ravens whom you saved from starving; when we had grown big, and heard that you were seeking the Golden Apple, we flew over the sea to the end of the world, where the Tree of Life stands, and have brought you the apple."

The youth, full of joy, set out homewards, and took the Golden Apple to the king's beautiful daughter, who had now no more excuses left to make. They cut the Apple of Life in two and ate it together; and then her heart became full of love for him, and they lived in undisturbed happiness to a great age.

# THE WATER OF LIFE

Long before you or I were born, there reigned, in a country a great way off, a king who had three sons. This king one day fell very ill—so ill that nobody thought he could live.

His sons were very much grieved at their father's sickness; and as they were walking together very mournfully in the garden of the palace, a little old man met them and asked what was the matter.

They told him that their father was very ill, and that they were afraid nothing could save him.

"I know what would," said the little old man; "it is the Water of Life. If he could have a draught of it he would be well again; but it is very hard to get."

Then the eldest son said, "I will soon find it," and he went to the sick king and begged that he might go in search of the Water of Life, as it was the only thing that could save him.

"No," said the king. "I had rather die than place you in such great danger as you must meet with in your journey."

But he begged so hard that the king let him go; and the prince thought to himself, "If I bring my father this water, he will make me sole heir to his kingdom."

Then he set out: and when he had gone on his way some time he came to a deep valley, overhung with rocks and woods; and as he looked around, he saw standing above him on one of the rocks a little ugly dwarf, with a sugarloaf cap and a scarlet cloak; and the dwarf called to him and said, "Prince, whither so fast?"

"What is that to thee, you ugly imp?" said the prince haughtily, and rode on.

But the dwarf was enraged at his behavior, and laid a fairy spell of ill luck upon him; so that as he rode on the mountain pass became narrower and narrower, and at last the way was so straitened that he could not go a step farther; and when he thought to have turned his horse round to go back the way he had come, he heard a loud laugh ringing round him, and found that the path was closed behind him, so that he was shut in all round.

He next tried to get off his horse and make his way on foot, but again the laugh rang in his ears, and he found himself unable to move a step, and thus he was forced to abide spellbound.

Meantime, the old king was lingering on in daily hope of his son's return, till at last the second son said, "Father, I will go in search of the Water of Life."

For he thought to himself, "My brother is surely dead, and the kingdom will fall to me if I find the water."

The king was at first very unwilling to let him go, but at last yielded to his wish. So he set out and followed the same road which his brother had done, and met with the same elf, who stopped him at the same spot in the mountains, saying, as before, "Prince, prince, whither so fast?"

"Mind your own affairs, busybody!" said the prince scornfully, and rode on.

But the dwarf put the same spell upon him as he put on his elder brother, and he, too, was at last obliged to take up his abode in the heart of the mountains.

Thus it is with proud silly people, who think themselves above everyone else, and are too proud to ask or take advice.

When the second prince had thus been gone a long time, the youngest son said he would go and search for the Water of Life, and trusted he should soon be able to make his father well again.

So he set out, and the dwarf met him too at the same spot in the valley, among the mountains, and said, "Prince, whither so fast?"

And the prince said, "I am going in search of the Water of Life, because my father is ill, and like to die; can you help me? Pray be kind, and aid me if you can!"

"Do you know where it is to be found?" asked the dwarf.

"No," said the prince, "I do not. Pray tell me if you know."

"Then as you have spoken to me kindly, and are wise enough to seek for advice, I will tell you how and where to go. The water you seek springs from a well in an enchanted castle; and, that you may be able to reach it in safety, I will give you an iron wand and two little loaves of bread; strike the iron door of the castle three times with the wand, and it will open; two hungry lions will be lying down inside gaping for their prey, but if you throw them the bread they will let you pass; then hasten on to the well, and take some of the Water of Life before the clock strikes twelve; for if you tarry longer the door will shut upon you forever."

Then the prince thanked his little friend with the scarlet cloak for his friendly aid, and took the wand and the bread, and went traveling on and on, over sea and over land, till he came to his journey's end, and found everything to be as the dwarf had told him. The door flew open at the third stroke of the wand, and when the lions were quieted he went on through the castle and came at length to a beautiful hall. Around it he saw several knights sitting in a trance; then he pulled off their rings and put them on his own fingers. In another room he saw on a table a sword and a loaf of bread, which he also took.

Farther on he came to a room where a beautiful young lady sat upon a couch; and she welcomed him joyfully, and said if he would set her free from the spell that bound her, the kingdom should be his, if he would come back in a year and marry her.

Then she told him that the well that held the Water of Life was in the palace gardens; and bade him make haste, and draw what he wanted before the clock struck twelve.

He walked on; and as he walked through beautiful gardens he came to a delightful shady spot in which stood a couch; and he thought to himself, as he felt tired, that he would rest himself for a while and gaze on the lovely scenes around him.

So he laid himself down, and sleep fell upon him unawares, so that he did not wake up till the clock was striking a quarter to twelve.

Then he sprang from the couch dreadfully frightened, ran to the well, filled a cup that was standing by him full of water, and hastened to get away in time.

Just as he was going out of the iron door it struck twelve, and the door fell so quickly upon him that it snapped off a piece of his heel.

When he found himself safe, he was overjoyed to think that he had got the Water of Life; and as he was going on his way homewards, he passed by the little dwarf, who, when he saw the sword and the loaf, said, "You have made a noble prize; with the sword you can at a blow slay whole armies, and the bread will never fail you."

Then the prince thought to himself, "I cannot go home to my father without my brothers"—so he said, "My dear friend, can you tell me where my two brothers are, who set out in search of the Water of Life before me and never came back?"

"I have shut them up by a charm between two mountains," said the dwarf, "because they were proud and ill-behaved, and scorned to ask advice."

The prince begged so hard for his brothers that the dwarf at last set them free, though unwillingly, saying, "Beware of them, for they have bad hearts."

Their brother, however, was greatly rejoiced to see them, and told them all that had happened to him; how he had found the Water of Life, and had taken a cup full of it; and how he had set a beautiful princess free from a spell that bound her; and how she had engaged to wait a whole year, and then to marry him, and to give him the kingdom.

*"My dear friend, can you tell me where my two brothers are?"*

Then they all three rode on together, and on their way home came to a country that was laid waste by war and a dreadful famine, so that it was feared all must die for want. But the prince gave the king of the land the bread, and all his kingdom ate of it. And he lent the king the wonderful sword, and he slew the enemy's army with it; and thus the kingdom was once more in peace and plenty. In the same manner he befriended two other countries through which they passed on their way.

When they came to the sea, they got into a ship and during their voyage the two eldest said to themselves, "Our brother has got the water which we could not find, therefore our father will forsake us and give him the kingdom, which is our right"; so they were full of envy and revenge, and agreed together how they could ruin him.

Then they waited till he was fast asleep, and poured the Water of Life out of the cup, and took it for themselves, giving him bitter seawater instead.

When they came to their journey's end, the youngest son brought his cup to the sick king, that he might drink and be healed.

Scarcely, however, had he tasted the bitter seawater than he became worse even than he was before; and then both the elder sons came in, and blamed the youngest for what they had done; and said that he wanted to poison their father, but that they had found the Water of Life, and had brought it with them. He no sooner began to drink of what they brought him, than he felt his sickness leave him, and was as strong and well as in his younger days.

Then they went to their brother, and laughed at him, and said, "Well, brother, you found the Water of Life, did you? You have had the trouble and we shall have the reward. Pray, with all your cleverness, why did not you manage to keep your eyes open?

"Next year one of us will take away your beautiful princess, if you do not take care. You had better say nothing about this to our father, for he does not believe a word you say; and if you tell tales, you shall lose your life into the bargain; but be quiet, and we will let you off."

The old king was still very angry with his youngest son, and thought that he really meant to have taken away his life; so he called his court together, and asked what should be done, and all agreed that he ought to be put to death.

The prince knew nothing of what was going on, till one day, when the king's chief huntsman went a-hunting with him, and they were alone in the wood together, the huntsman looked so sorrowful that the prince said, "My friend, what is the matter with you?"

"I cannot and dare not tell you," said he.

But the prince begged very hard, and said, "Only tell me what it is, and do not think I shall be angry, for I will forgive you."

"Alas!" said the huntsman; "the king has ordered me to shoot you."

The prince started at this, and said, "Let me live, and I will change dresses with you; you shall take my royal coat to show to my father, and do you give me your shabby one."

"With all my heart," said the huntsman; "I am sure I shall be glad to save you, for I could not have shot you."

Then he took the prince's coat, and gave him the shabby one, and went away through the wood.

Some time after, three grand embassies came to the old king's court, with rich gifts of gold and precious stones for his youngest son; now all these were sent from the three kings to whom he had lent his sword and loaf of bread, in order to rid them of their enemy and feed their people.

This touched the old king's heart, and he thought his son might still be guiltless, and said to his court, "Oh that my son were still alive! How it grieves me that I had him killed!"

"He is still alive," said the huntsman; "and I am glad that I had pity on him, but let him go in peace, and brought home his royal coat."

At this the king was overwhelmed with joy, and made it known throughout all his kingdom that if his son would come back to his court he would forgive him.

Meanwhile the princess was eagerly waiting till her deliverer should come back; and had a road made leading up to her palace all of shining gold; and told her courtiers that whoever came on horseback, and rode straight up to the gate upon it, was her true lover, and they must let him in; but whoever rode on one side of it, they must be sure was not the right one, and they must send him away at once.

The time soon came when the eldest brother thought that he would make haste to go to the princess and say that he was the one who had set her free, and that he should have her for his wife, and the kingdom with her.

As he came before the palace and saw the golden road, he stopped to look at it, and he thought to himself, "It is a pity to ride upon this beautiful road"; so he turned aside and rode on the right-hand side of it. But when he came to the gate, the guards, who had seen the road he took, said to him that he could not be who he said he was, and must go about his business.

The second prince set out soon afterwards on the same errand; and when he came to the golden road, and his horse had set one foot upon it, he stopped to look at it, and thought it very beautiful, and said to himself, "What a pity it is that anything should tread here!" Then he too turned aside and rode on the left side of it. But when he came to the gate the guards said he was not the true prince, and that he too must go away about his business; and away he went.

Now when the full year was come round, the third brother left the forest in which he had lain hid for fear of his father's anger, and set out in search of his betrothed bride.

So he journeyed on, thinking of her all the way, and rode so quickly that he did not even see what the road was made of, but went with his horse straight over it; and as he came to the gate it flew open, and the princess welcomed him with joy, and said he was her deliverer, and he should now be her husband and lord of the kingdom. When the first joy at their meeting was over, the princess told him she had heard of his father having forgiven him, and of his wish to have him home again; so, before his wedding with the princess, he went to visit his father, taking her with him.

Then he told him everything—how his brothers had cheated and robbed him, and yet that he had borne all those wrongs for the love of his father. And the old king was very angry, and wanted to punish his wicked sons; but they made their escape, and got into a ship and sailed away over the wide sea, and where they went to nobody knew and nobody cared.

And now the old king gathered together his court, and asked all his kingdom to come and celebrate the wedding of his son and the princess. And young and old, noble and squire, gentle and simple, came at once on the summons; and among the rest came the friendly dwarf, with the sugarloaf hat, and a new scarlet cloak.

And the wedding was held, and the merry bells rung, and all the good people they danced and they sang, and feasted and frolicked I can't tell how long.

195

*"Whoever has stolen one of my roses shall be eaten up alive!"*

# BEAUTY AND THE BEAST

Amerchant, who had three daughters, was once setting out upon a journey; but before he went he asked each daughter what gift he should bring back for her. The eldest wished for pearls; the second for jewels; but the third, who was called Lily, said, "Dear father, bring me a rose."

Now it was no easy task to find a rose, for it was the middle of winter; yet as she was his prettiest daughter, and was very fond of flowers, her father said he would see what he could do. So he kissed all three, and bid them goodbye.

And when the time came for him to go home, he had bought pearls and jewels for the two eldest, but he had sought everywhere in vain for the rose; and when he went into any garden and asked for such a thing, the people laughed at him, and asked him whether he thought roses grew in snow.

This grieved him very much, for Lily was his dearest child; and as he was journeying home, thinking what he should bring her, he came to a fine castle; and around the castle was a garden, in one half of which it seemed to be summertime and in the other half winter. On one side the finest flowers were in full bloom, and on the other everything looked dreary and buried in the snow.

"A lucky find!" said he, and he called to his servant and told him to go to a beautiful bed of roses that was there and bring him away one of the finest flowers.

This done, they were riding away well pleased, when up sprang a fierce lion, and roared out, "Whoever has stolen one of my roses shall be eaten up alive!"

Then the man said, "I knew not that the garden belonged to you; can nothing save my life?"

"No!" said the lion, "nothing, unless you undertake to give me whatever meets you on your return home; if you agree to this, I will give you your life, and the rose too for your daughter."

But the man was unwilling to do so and said, "It may be my youngest daughter, who loves me most, and always runs to meet me when I go home."

Then the servant was greatly frightened, and said, "It may perhaps be only a cat or a dog."

And at last the man yielded with a heavy heart, and took the rose; and said he would give the lion whatever should meet him first on his return.

And as he came near home, it was Lily, his youngest and dearest daughter, that met him; she came running, and kissed him, and welcomed him home; and when she saw that he had brought her the rose, she was still more glad.

But her father began to be very sorrowful, and to weep, saying, "Alas, my dearest child! I have bought this flower at a high price, for I have said I would give you to a wild lion; and when he has you, he will tear you in pieces, and eat you."

Then he told her all that had happened, and said she should not go, come what may.

But she comforted him, and said, "Dear father, the word you have given must be kept; I will go to the lion, and soothe him; perhaps he will let me come safe home again."

The next morning she asked the way she was to go, and took leave of her father, and went forth with a bold heart into the wood. But the lion was an enchanted prince. By day he and all his court were lions, but in the evening they took their right forms again.

And when Lily came to the castle, he welcomed her so courteously that she agreed to marry him. The wedding feast was held, and they lived happily together a long time. The prince was only to be seen as soon as evening came, and then he held his court; but every morning he left his bride, and went away by himself, she knew not whither, till the night came again.

After some time he said to her, "Tomorrow there will be a great feast in your father's house, for your eldest sister is to be married; and if you wish to go and visit her my lions shall lead you thither."

Then she rejoiced much at the thought of seeing her father once more, and set out with the lions; and everyone was overjoyed to see her, for they had thought her dead long since. But she told them how happy she was, and stayed till the feast was over, and then went back to the wood.

Her second sister was soon after married, and when Lily was asked to go to the wedding, she said to the prince, "I will not go alone this time—you must go with me."

But he would not, and explained that it would be a very hazardous thing, for if the least ray of the torchlight should fall upon him his enchantment would become still worse: he should be changed into a dove, and be forced to wander about the world for seven long years.

However, she gave him no rest, and said she would take care no light should fall upon him. So at last they set out together, and took with them their little child; and she chose a large hall with thick walls for him to sit in while the wedding torches were lighted; but, unluckily, no one saw that there was a crack in the door. Then the wedding was held with great pomp, but as the train came from the church, and passed with the torches before the hall, a very small ray of light fell upon the prince. In a moment he disappeared, and when his wife came in and looked for him, she found only a white dove; and it said to her, "Seven years must I fly up and down over the face of the earth, but every now and then I will let fall a white feather that will show you the way I am going; follow it, and at last you may overtake and set me free."

*Lily and the lions.*

This said, he flew out at the door, and poor Lily followed; and every now and then a white feather fell, and showed her the way she was to journey.

Thus she went roving on through the wide world, and looked neither to the right hand nor to the left, nor took any rest, for seven years. Then she began to be glad, and thought to herself that the time was fast coming when all her troubles should end; yet repose was still far off, for one day as she was traveling on she missed the white feather, and when she lifted up her eyes she could nowhere see the dove. "Now," thought she to herself, "no aid of man can be of use to me."

So she went to the sun and said, "Thou shinest everywhere, on the hill's top and the valley's depth—hast thou anywhere seen my white dove?"

"No," said the sun, "I have not seen it; but I will give thee a casket—open it when thy hour of need comes."

So she thanked the sun, and went on her way till eventide; and when the moon arose, she cried unto it, and said, "Thou shinest through the night, over field and grove—hast thou nowhere seen my white dove?"

"No," said the moon, "I cannot help thee; but I will give thee an egg—break it when need comes."

Then she thanked the moon, and went on till the night wind blew; and she raised up her voice to it, and said, "Thou blowest through every tree and under every leaf—hast thou not seen my white dove?"

"No," said the night wind, "but I will ask three other winds; perhaps they have seen it."

Then the east wind and the west wind came, and said they too had not seen it, but the south wind said, "I have seen the white dove—he has fled to the Red Sea, and is changed once more into a lion, for the seven years are passed away, and there he is fighting with a dragon; and the dragon is an enchanted princess, who seeks to separate him from you."

Then the night wind said, "I will give thee counsel. Go to the Red Sea; on the right shore stand many rods: count them, and when thou comest to the eleventh, break it off, and smite the dragon with it; and so the lion will have the victory, and both of them will appear to you in their own forms.

"Then look round and thou wilt see a winged griffin, sitting by the Red Sea; jump onto his back with thy beloved one as quickly as possible, and he will carry you over the waters to your home. I will also give thee this nut," continued the night wind. "When you are halfway over, throw it down, and out of the waters will immediately spring up a high nut tree on which the griffin will be able to rest, otherwise he would not have the strength to bear you the whole way; if, therefore, thou dost forget to throw down the nut, he will let you both fall into the sea."

So our poor wanderer went forth, and found all as the night wind had said; and she plucked the eleventh rod, and smote the dragon, and the lion forthwith became a prince and the dragon a princess again.

But no sooner was the princess released from the spell, than she seized the prince by the arm and sprang onto the griffin's back, and went off carrying the prince away with her.

Thus the unhappy traveler was again forsaken and forlorn; but she took heart and said, "As far as the wind blows, and so long as the cock crows, I will journey on till I find him once again."

She went on for a long, long way, till at length she came to the castle whither the princess had carried the prince; and there was a feast got ready, and she heard that the wedding was about to be held. "Heaven aid me now!" said she; and she took the casket that the sun had given her, and found that within it lay a dress as dazzling as the sun itself.

So she put it on, and went into the palace, and all the people gazed upon her; and the dress pleased the bride so much that she asked whether it was to be sold. "Not for gold and silver," said she, "but for flesh and blood."

The princess asked what she meant, and she said, "Let me speak with the bridegroom this night in his chamber, and I will give thee the dress."

At last the princess agreed, but she told her chamberlain to give the prince a sleeping draught, that he might not hear or see her. When evening came, and the prince had fallen asleep, she was led into his chamber, and she sat herself down at his feet, and said: "I have followed thee seven years. I have been to the sun, the moon, and the night wind, to seek thee, and at last I have helped thee to overcome the dragon. Wilt thou then forget me quite?"

But the prince all the time slept so soundly, that her voice only passed over him, and seemed like the whistling of the wind among the fir trees.

Then poor Lily was led away, and forced to give up the golden dress; and when she saw that there was no help for her, she went out into a meadow, and sat herself down and wept.

But as she sat she bethought herself of the egg that the moon had given her; and when she broke it, there ran out a hen and twelve chickens of pure gold, that played about, and then nestled under the old one's wings, so as to form the most beautiful sight in the world.

And she rose up and drove them before her, till the bride saw them from her window, and was so pleased that she came forth and asked her if she would sell the brood. "Not for gold or silver, but for flesh and blood: let me again this evening speak with the bridegroom in his chamber, and I will give thee the whole brood."

Then the princess thought to betray her as before, and agreed to what she asked; but when the prince went to his chamber he asked the chamberlain why the wind had whistled so in the night. And the chamberlain told him all—how he had given him a sleeping draught, and how a poor maiden had come and spoken to him in his chamber, and was to come again that night.

Then the prince took care to throw away the sleeping draught; and when Lily came and began again to tell him what woes had befallen her, and how faithful and true to him she had been, he knew his beloved wife's voice, and sprang up, and said, "You have awakened me as from a dream, for the strange princess had thrown a spell around me, so that I had altogether forgotten you; but heaven hath sent you to me in a lucky hour."

And they stole away out of the palace by night unawares, and seated themselves on the griffin, who flew back with them over the Red Sea.

When they were halfway across Lily let the nut fall into the water, and immediately a large nut tree arose from the sea, whereon the griffin rested for a while, and then carried them safely home. There they found their child, now grown up to be comely and fair; and after all their troubles they lived happily together to the end of their days.

# THE GOLDEN GOOSE

There was a man who had three sons, the youngest of whom was called Simpleton and was despised, mocked, and sneered at on every occasion.

It happened that the eldest wanted to go into the forest to hew wood, and before he went his mother gave him a beautiful sweet cake and a bottle of wine in order that he might not suffer from hunger or thirst.

When he entered the forest he met a little gray-haired old man who bade him good day, and said: "Do give me a piece of cake out of your pocket, and let me have a draught of your wine; I am so hungry and thirsty."

But the clever son answered: "If I give you my cake and wine, I shall have none for myself; be off with you," and he left the little man standing and went on.

But when he began to hew down a tree, it was not long before he made a false stroke, and the axe cut him in the arm, so that he had to go home and have it bound up. And this was the little gray man's doing.

After this the second son went into the forest, and his mother gave him, like the eldest, a cake and a bottle of wine.

The little old gray man met him likewise, and asked him for a piece of cake and a drink of wine. But the second son, too, said sensibly enough: "What I give you will be taken away from myself; be off!" and he left the little man standing and went on.

His punishment, however, was not delayed; when he had made a few blows at the tree he struck himself in the leg, so that he had to be carried home.

Then Simpleton said: "Father, do let me go and cut wood."

The father answered: "Your brothers have hurt themselves with it; leave it alone, you do not understand anything about it."

But Simpleton begged so long that at last he said: "Just go then, you will get wiser by hurting yourself." His mother gave him a cake made with water and baked in the cinders, and with it a bottle of sour beer.

When he came to the forest the little old gray man met him likewise, and greeting him, said: "Give me a piece of your cake and a drink out of your bottle; I am so hungry and thirsty."

Simpleton answered: "I have only cinder cake and sour beer; if that pleases you, we will sit down and eat."

So they sat down, and when Simpleton pulled out his cinder cake, it was a fine sweet cake, and the sour beer had become good wine.

So they ate and drank, and after that the little man said: "Since you have a good heart, and are willing to divide what you have, I will give you good luck. There stands an old tree; cut it down, and you will find something at the roots." Then the little man took leave of him.

Simpleton went and cut down the tree, and when it fell there was a goose sitting in the roots with feathers of pure gold. He lifted her up, and taking her with him, went to an inn where he thought he would stay the night.

Now the host had three daughters, who saw the goose and were curious to know what such a wonderful bird might be, and would have liked to have one of its golden feathers.

The eldest thought: "I shall soon find an opportunity of pulling out a feather," and as soon as Simpleton had gone out she seized the goose by the wing, but her hand remained sticking fast to it.

The second came soon afterwards, thinking only of how she might get a feather for herself, but she had scarcely touched her sister than she was held fast.

At last the third also came with the like intent, and the others screamed out: "Keep away; for goodness' sake, keep away!"

But she did not understand why she was to keep away. "The others are there," she thought, "I may as well be there too," and ran to them; but as soon as she had touched her sister, she remained sticking fast to her. So they had to spend the night with the goose.

The next morning Simpleton took the goose under his arm and set out, without troubling himself about the three girls who were hanging on to it. They were obliged to run after him continually, now left, now right, wherever his legs took him.

In the middle of the fields the parson met them, and when he saw

the procession he said: "For shame, you good-for-nothing girls, why are you running across the fields after this young man? Is that seemly?"

At the same time he seized the youngest by the hand in order to pull her away, but as soon as he touched her he likewise stuck fast, and was himself obliged to run behind.

Before long the sexton came by and saw his master, the parson, running behind three girls. He was astonished at this and called out: "Hi! Your reverence, whither away so quickly? Do not forget that we have a christening today!" and running after him he took him by the sleeve, but was also held fast to it.

While the five were trotting thus, one behind the other, two laborers came with their hoes from the fields; the parson called out to them

and begged that they would set him and the sexton free. But they had scarcely touched the sexton when they were held fast, and now there were seven of them running behind Simpleton and the goose.

Soon afterwards he came to a city, where a king ruled who had a daughter who was so serious that no one could make her laugh. So her father had put forth a decree that whosoever should be able to make her laugh should marry her.

When Simpleton heard this, he went with his goose and all her train before the king's daughter, and as soon as she saw the seven people running on and on, one behind the other, she began to laugh quite loudly and as if she would never stop. Thereupon Simpleton asked to have her for his wife; but the king did not want him for a son-in-law, and made all manner of excuses and said he must first produce a man who could drink a cellarful of wine.

Simpleton thought of the little gray man, who could certainly help him; so he went into the forest, and in the same place where he had felled the tree, he saw a man sitting, who had a very sorrowful face.

Simpleton asked him what he was taking to heart so sorely, and he answered: "I have such a great thirst and cannot quench it; cold water I cannot stand, a barrel of wine I have just emptied, but that to me is like a drop on a hot stone!"

"There I can help you," said Simpleton, "just come with me and you shall be satisfied."

He led him into the king's cellar, and the man bent over the huge barrels and drank till his loins hurt, and before the day was out he had emptied all the barrels.

Then Simpleton asked once more for his bride, but the king was vexed that such an ugly fellow, whom everyone called Simpleton, should take away his daughter, and he made a new condition; he must first find a man who could eat a whole mountain of bread.

Simpleton did not think long, but went straight into the forest, where in the same place there sat a man who was tying up his body with a strap, and making an awful face, and saying: "I have eaten a whole ovenful of rolls, but what good is that when one has such a hunger as I? My stomach remains empty, and I must tie myself up if I am not to die of hunger."

At this Simpleton was glad, and said: "Get up and come with me; you shall eat yourself full."

He led him to the king's palace where all the flour in the whole kingdom was collected, and from it he caused a huge mountain of bread to be baked.

The man from the forest stood before it, began to eat, and by the end of one day the whole mountain had vanished.

Then Simpleton for the third time asked for his bride; but the king again sought a way out, and ordered him to find a ship which could sail on land and on water.

"As soon as you come sailing back in it," said he, "you shall have my daughter for wife."

Simpleton went straight into the forest, and there sat the little gray man to whom he had given his cake.

When he heard what Simpleton wanted, he said: "Since you have given me to eat and to drink, I will give you the ship; and I do all this because you once were kind to me."

Then he gave him the ship which could sail on land and water, and when the king saw that, he could no longer prevent him from having his daughter.

The wedding was celebrated, and after the king's death, Simpleton inherited his kingdom and lived for a long time contentedly with his wife.

*Then the fiddler went his way, and took her with him.*

# KING GRISLY BEARD

A great king of a land far away in the east had a daughter who was very beautiful, but so proud, and haughty, and conceited, that none of the princes who came to ask her in marriage was good enough for her, and she only made sport of them.

Once upon a time the king held a great feast, and asked thither all her suitors; and they all sat in a row, ranged according to their rank—kings, and princes, and dukes, and earls, and counts, and barons, and knights. Then the princess came in, and as she passed by them she had something spiteful to say to everyone. The first was too fat: "He's as round as a tub," said she. The next was too tall: "What a maypole!" said she. The next was too short: "What a dumpling!" said she. The fourth was too pale, and she called him "Wallface." The fifth was too red, so she called him "Coxcomb." The sixth was not straight enough, so she said he was like a green stick that had been laid to dry over a baker's oven. And thus she had some joke to crack about everyone; but she laughed more than all at a good king who was there. "Look at him," said she; "his beard is like an old mop; he shall be called Grisly Beard." So the king got the nickname of Grisly Beard.

But the old king was very angry when he saw how his daughter behaved, and how she ill-treated all his guests; and he vowed that, willing or unwilling, she should marry the first man, be he prince or beggar, that next came to the door.

Two days after there came by a traveling fiddler, who began to play under the window and beg alms; and when the king heard him, he said, "Let him come in." So they brought in a dirty-looking fellow; and when he had sung before the king and the princess, he begged a boon. Then the king said, "You have sung so well, that I will give you my daughter for your wife." The princess begged and prayed; but the king said, "I have sworn to give you to the first comer, and I will keep my word." So words and tears were of no avail; the parson was sent for, and she was married to the fiddler. When this was over the king said, "Now you must travel on with your husband."

Then the fiddler went his way, and took her with him, and they soon came to a great wood. "Pray," said she, "whose is this wood?"

"It belongs to King Grisly Beard," answered he; "hadst thou taken him, all had been thine."

"Ah! unlucky wretch that I am!" sighed she; "would that I had married King Grisly Beard!"

Next they came to some fine meadows. "Whose are these beautiful green meadows?" said she.

"They belong to King Grisly Beard, hadst thou taken him, they had all been thine."

"Ah! unlucky wretch that I am!" said she; "would that I had married King Grisly Beard!"

Then they came to a great city. "Whose is this noble city?" said she.

"It belongs to King Grisly Beard; hadst thou taken him, it had all been thine."

"Ah! wretch that I am!" sighed she; "why did I not marry King Grisly Beard?"

"That is no business of mine," said the fiddler; "why should you wish for another husband? Am not I good enough for you?"

At last they came to a small cottage. "What a paltry place!" said she; "to whom does that little dirty hole belong?"

Then the fiddler said, "That is your and my house, where we will live."

"Where are your servants?" cried she.

"What do we want with servants?" said he; "you must do for yourself whatever is to be done. Now make the fire, and put on water and cook my supper, for I am very tired."

But the princess knew nothing of making fires and cooking, and the fiddler was forced to help her. When they had eaten a very scanty meal they went to bed; but the fiddler made her get up very early in the morning to clean the house. Thus they lived for two days; and when they had eaten up all there was in the cottage, the man said, "Wife, we can't go on thus, spending money and earning nothing. You must learn to weave baskets." Then he went out and cut willows, and brought them home, and she began to weave; but it made her fingers very sore. "I see this work won't do," said he; "try and spin, perhaps you will do that better." So she sat down and tried to spin; but the threads cut her tender fingers till the blood ran. "See now," said the fiddler, "you are good for nothing; you can do no work: what a bargain I have got! However, I'll try and set up a trade in pots and pans, and you shall stand in the market and sell them."

"Alas!" sighed she, "if any of my father's court should pass by and see me standing in the market, how they will laugh at me!"

But her husband did not care for that, and said she must work if she did not wish to die of hunger. At first the trade went well; for many people, seeing such a beautiful woman, went to buy her wares, and paid their money without thinking of taking away the goods. They lived on this as long as it lasted; and then her husband bought a fresh lot of ware, and she sat herself down with it in the corner of the market; but a drunken soldier soon came by, and rode his horse against her stall, and broke all her goods into a thousand pieces.

Then she began to cry, and knew not what to do. "Ah! What will become of me?" said she; "what will my husband say?" So she ran home and told him all.

"Who would have thought you would have been so silly," said he, "as to put an earthenware stall in the corner of the market, where everybody passes? But let us have no more crying; I see you are not fit for this sort of work, so I have been to the king's palace, and asked if they want a kitchen maid; and they say they will take you, and there you will have plenty to eat."

Thus the princess became a kitchen maid, and helped the cook to do all the dirtiest work; but she was allowed to carry home some of the meat that was left, and on this they lived.

She had not been there long before she heard that the king's eldest son was passing by, going to be married; and she went to one of the windows and looked out. Everything was ready, and all the pomp and brightness of the court was there. Then she bitterly grieved for the pride and folly which had brought her so low. And the servants gave her some of the rich meats, which she put into her basket to take home.

All on a sudden, as she was going out, in came the king's son in golden clothes; and when he saw a beautiful woman at the door, he took her by the hand, and said she should be his partner in the dance; but she trembled for fear, for she saw that it was King Grisly Beard, who was making sport of her. However, he kept fast hold, and led her in; and the cover of the basket came off, so that the meats in it fell about. Then everybody laughed and jeered at her; and she was so abashed that she wished herself a thousand feet deep in the earth. She sprang to the door to run away; but on the steps King Grisly Beard overtook her, and brought her back and said, "Fear me not! I am the fiddler who has lived with you in the hut. I brought you there because I really loved you. I am also the soldier that overset your stall. I have done all this only to cure you of your silly pride, and to show you the folly of your ill treatment of me. Now all is over: you have learnt wisdom, and it is time to hold our marriage feast."

Then the chamberlains came and brought her the most beautiful robes; and her father and his whole court were there already, and welcomed her home on her marriage. Joy was in every face and every heart. The feast was grand; they danced and sang; all were merry; and I only wish that you and I had been of the party.

# THE KING OF THE
# GOLDEN MOUNTAIN

There was once a merchant who had only one child, a son, who was very young and barely able to run alone. He had two richly laden ships then making a voyage upon the seas, in which he had embarked all his wealth, in the hope of making great gains, but news came that both were lost. Thus from being a rich man he became all at once so very poor that nothing was left to him but one small plot of land; and there he often went in an evening to take his walk, and ease his mind of a little of his trouble.

One day, as he was roaming along in a brown study, thinking with no great comfort on what he had been and what he now was and was likely to be, all of a sudden there stood before him a little, rough-looking black dwarf.

"Prithee, friend, why so sorrowful?" said he to the merchant; "what is it you take so deeply to heart?"

"If you would do me any good I would willingly tell you," said the merchant.

"Who knows but I may?" said the little man. "Tell me what ails you, and perhaps you will find I may be of some use."

Then the merchant told him how all his wealth was gone to the bottom of the sea, and how he had nothing left but that little plot of land.

"Oh, trouble not yourself about that," said the dwarf; "only undertake to bring me here, twelve years hence, whatever meets you first on your going home, and I will give you as much as you please."

The merchant thought this was no great thing to ask; that it would most likely be his dog or his cat, or something of that sort, but forgot his little boy Heinel; so he agreed to the bargain, and signed and sealed the bond to do what was asked of him.

But as he drew near home, his little boy was so glad to see him that he crept behind him, and laid fast hold of his legs, and looked up in his face and laughed.

Then the father started, trembling with fear and horror, and saw what it was that he had bound himself to do; but as no gold was come, he made himself easy by thinking that it was only a joke that the dwarf was playing him, and that, at any rate, when the money came, he should see the bearer, and would not take it in.

About a month afterwards he went upstairs into a lumber room to look for some old iron, that he might sell it and raise a little money; and there, instead of his iron, he saw a large pile of gold lying on the floor.

At the sight of this he was overjoyed, and forgetting all about his son, went into trade again, and became a richer merchant than before.

Meantime little Heinel grew up, and as the end of the twelve years drew near the merchant began to call to mind his bond, and became very sad and thoughtful; so that care and sorrow were written upon his face.

The boy one day asked what was the matter, but his father would not tell for some time; at last, however, he said that he had, without knowing it, sold him for gold to a little, ugly-looking black dwarf, and that the twelve years were coming round when he must keep his word.

Then Heinel said, "Father, give yourself very little trouble about that; I shall be too much for the little man."

When the time came, the father and son went out together to the place agreed upon, and the son drew a circle on the ground and set

*The little black dwarf soon came, and walked round and round about the circle.*

himself and his father in the middle of it. The little black dwarf soon came, and walked round and round about the circle, but could not find any way to get into it, and he either could not or dared not jump over it.

At last the boy said to him. "Have you anything to say to us, my friend? What do you want?" Now Heinel had found a friend in a good fairy, that was fond of him, and had told him what to do; for this fairy knew what good luck was in store for him.

"Have you brought me what you said you would?" said the dwarf to the merchant.

The old man held his tongue, but Heinel said again, "What do you want here?"

The dwarf said, "I come to talk with your father, not with you."

"You have cheated and taken in my father," said the son; "pray give him up his bond at once."

"Fair and softly," said the little old man; "right is right; I have paid my money, and your father has had it, and spent it; so be so good as to let me have what I paid it for."

"You must have my consent to that first," said Heinel, "so please to step in here, and let us talk it over."

The old man grinned, and showed his teeth, as if he should have been very glad to get into the circle if he could. Then at last, after a long talk, they came to terms. Heinel agreed that his father must give him up, and that so far the dwarf should have his way; but, on the other hand, the fairy had told Heinel what fortune was in store for him if he followed his own course; and he did not choose to be given up to his humpbacked friend, who seemed so anxious for his company.

So, to make a sort of drawn battle of the matter, it was settled that Heinel should be put into an open boat that lay on the seashore hard by; that the father should push him off with his own hand, and that he should thus be set adrift, and left to the bad or good luck of wind and weather. Then he took leave of his father, and set himself in the boat, but before it got far off a wave struck it, and it fell with one side low in the water, so the merchant thought that poor Heinel was lost, and went home very sorrowful, while the dwarf went his way, thinking that at any rate he had had his revenge.

The boat, however, did not sink, for the good fairy took care of her friend, and soon raised the boat up again, and it went safely on. The young man sat safe within, till at length it ran ashore upon an unknown land. As he jumped upon the shore he saw before him a beautiful castle, but empty and dreary within, for it was enchanted. "Here," said he to himself, "must I find the prize the good fairy told me of." So he searched the whole palace through, till at last he found a white snake, lying coiled up on a cushion in one of the chambers.

Now the white snake was an enchanted princess; and she was very glad to see him, and said, "Are you at last come to set me free? Twelve long years have I waited here for the fairy to bring you hither as she promised, for you alone can save me. This night twelve men will come: their faces will be black, and they will be dressed in chain armor. They will ask what you do here, but give no answer; and let them do what they will—beat, whip, pinch, prick, or torment you—bear all; only speak not a word, and at twelve o'clock they must go away. The second night twelve others will come; and the third night twenty-four, who will even cut off your head; but at the twelfth hour of that night their power will be gone, and I shall be free, and will come and bring you the Water of Life, and will wash you with it, and bring you back to life and health." And all came to pass as she had said; Heinel bore all, and spoke not a word; and the third night the princess came, and fell on his neck and kissed him. Joy and gladness burst forth throughout the castle, the wedding was celebrated, and he was crowned King of the Golden Mountain.

They lived together very happily, and the queen had a son. And thus eight years had passed over their heads, when the king thought of his father; and he began to long to see him once again. But the queen was against his going, and said, "I know well that misfortunes will come upon us if you go." However, he gave her no rest till she agreed. At his going away she gave him a wishing ring, and said, "Take this ring, and put it on your finger; whatever you wish it will bring you; only promise never to make use of it to bring me hence to your father's house." Then he said he would do what she asked, and put the ring on his finger, and wished himself near the town where his father lived.

Heinel found himself at the gates in a moment; but the guards would not let him go in, because he was so strangely clad. So he went up to a neighboring hill, where a shepherd dwelt, and borrowed his old smock, and thus passed unknown into the town. When he came to his father's house, he said he was his son; but the merchant would not believe him, and said he had had but one son, his poor Heinel, who he knew was long since dead; and as he was only dressed like a poor shepherd, he would not even give him anything to eat. The king, however, still vowed that he was his son, and said, "Is there no mark by which you would know that I am really your son?"

"Yes," said his mother, "our Heinel had a mark like a raspberry on his right arm." Then he showed them the mark, and they knew that what he had said was true.

He next told them how he was King of the Golden Mountain, and was married to a princess, and had a son seven years old.

But the merchant said, "That can never be true; he must be a fine king truly who travels about in a shepherd's smock!"

At this the son was vexed; and forgetting his word, turned his ring and wished for his queen and son. In an instant they stood before him; but the queen wept, and said he had broken his word, and bad luck would follow. He did all he could to soothe her, and she at last seemed to be appeased; but she was not so in truth, and was only thinking how she should punish him.

One day he took her to walk with him out of the town, and showed her the spot where the boat was set adrift upon the wide waters. Then he sat himself down, and said, "I am very much tired; sit by me, I will rest my head in your lap, and sleep a while." As soon as he had fallen asleep, however, she drew the ring from his finger, and crept softly away, and wished herself and her son at home in their kingdom. And when he awoke he found himself alone, and saw that the ring was gone from his finger. "I can never go back to my father's house," said he; "they would say I am a sorcerer. I will journey forth into the world, till I come again to my kingdom."

So saying he set out and traveled till he came to a hill where three giants were sharing their father's goods; and as they saw him pass they cried out and said, "Little men have sharp wits; he shall part the goods between us." Now there was a sword that cut off an enemy's head whenever the wearer gave the words "Heads off!"; a cloak that made the owner invisible, or gave him any form he pleased; and a pair of boots that carried the wearer wherever he wished. Heinel said they must first let him try these wonderful things, then he might know how to set a value upon them. Then they gave him the cloak, and he wished himself a fly, and in a moment he was a fly. "The cloak is very well," said he; "now give me the sword."

"No," said they; "not unless you undertake not to say 'Heads off!' for if you do we are all dead men." So they gave it him, charging him to try it on a tree. He next asked for the boots also; and the moment he had all three in his power, he wished himself at the Golden Mountain; and there he was at once. So the giants were left behind with no goods to share or quarrel about.

As Heinel came near his castle he heard the sound of merry music; and the people around told him that his queen was about to marry another husband. Then he threw his cloak around him, and passed through the castle hall, and placed himself by the side of the queen, where no one saw him.

But when anything to eat was put upon her plate, he took it away and ate it himself; and when a glass of wine was handed to her, he took it and drank it; and thus, though they kept on giving her meat and drink, her plate and cup were always empty.

Upon this, fear and remorse came over her, and she went into her chamber alone, and sat there weeping; and he followed her there. "Alas!" said she to herself, "was I not once set free? Why then does this enchantment still seem to bind me?"

"False and fickle one!" said he. "One indeed came who set thee free, and he is now near thee again; but how have you used him? Ought he to have had such treatment from thee?"

Then he went out and sent away the company, and said the wedding was at an end now that he had come back to his kingdom. But the princes, peers, and great men mocked at him. However, he would enter into no parley with them, but only asked them if they would go in peace or not. Then they turned upon him and tried to seize him; but he drew his sword. "Heads off!" cried he; and with the word the traitors' heads fell before him, and Heinel was once more King of the Golden Mountain.

# THE SEVEN RAVENS

There was once a man who had seven sons, and last of all one daughter. Although the little girl was very pretty, she was so weak and small that they thought she could not live and they said she should at once be christened.

So the father sent one of his sons in haste to the spring to get some water, but the other six ran with him. Each wanted to be first at drawing the water, and so they were in such a hurry that all let their pitchers fall into the well, and they stood very foolishly looking at one another, and did not know what to do, for none dared go home.

In the meantime the father was uneasy, and could not tell what made the young men stay so long. "Surely," said he, "the whole seven must have forgotten themselves over some game of play"—and when he had waited still longer and they yet did not come, he flew into a rage and wished them all turned into ravens.

Scarcely had he spoken these words when he heard a croaking over his head, and looked up and saw seven ravens as black as coal flying round and round. Sorry as he was to see his wish so fulfilled, he did not know how what was done could be undone, and comforted himself as well as he could for the loss of his seven sons with his dear little daughter, who soon became stronger and every day more beautiful.

For a long time she did not know that she had ever had any brothers, for her father and mother took care not to speak of them before her; but one day by chance she heard the people about her speak of them.

"Yes," said they, "she is beautiful indeed, but still 'tis a pity that her brothers should have been lost for her sake."

Then she was much grieved, and went to her father and mother, and asked if she had had any brothers, and what had become of them. So they dared no longer hide the truth from her, but said it was the will of heaven, and that her birth was only the innocent cause of it; but the little girl mourned sadly about it every day, and thought herself bound to do all she could to bring her brothers back; and she had neither rest nor ease, till at length one day she stole away, and set out into the wide world to find her brothers, wherever they might be, and free them, whatever it might cost her.

She took nothing with her but a little ring which her father and mother had given her, a loaf of bread in case she should be hungry, a little pitcher of water in case she should be thirsty, and a little stool to rest upon when she should be weary.

Thus she went on and on, and journeyed till she came to the world's end; then she came to the sun, but the sun looked much too hot and fiery; so she ran away quickly to the moon, but the moon was cold and chilly, and said, "I smell flesh and blood this way!"

So she took herself away in a hurry and came to the stars, and the stars were friendly and kind to her, and each star sat upon his own little stool; but the morning star rose up and gave her a little piece of wood, and said, "If you have not this little piece of wood, you cannot unlock the castle that stands on the glass mountain; it is there your brothers live."

The little girl took the piece of wood, rolled it up in a little cloth, and went on again until she came to the glass mountain, and found the door to the castle shut. Then she felt for the little piece of wood; but when she unwrapped the cloth it was not there, and she saw she had lost the gift of the good stars.

What was to be done? She wanted to save her brothers but had no key to the castle of the glass mountain; so this faithful little sister took a

*She put it in the door and opened it.*

knife out of her pocket and cut off her little finger, that was just the size of the piece of wood she had lost, and put it in the door and opened it.

As she went in, a little dwarf came up to her, and said, "What are you seeking for?"

"I seek for my brothers, the seven ravens," answered she.

Then the dwarf said, "My masters are not at home; but if you will wait till they come, pray step in."

Now the little dwarf was getting their dinner ready, and he brought their food upon seven little plates, and their drink in seven little glasses, and set them upon the table, and out of each little plate their sister ate a small piece, and out of each little glass she drank a small drop; but she let the ring that she had brought with her fall into the last glass.

All of a sudden she heard a fluttering and croaking in the air, and the dwarf said, "Here come my masters."

When they came in, they wanted to eat and drink, and looked for their little plates and glasses.

Then said one after the other, "Who has eaten from my little plate? And who has been drinking out of my little glass? Caw! Caw! Well I ween mortal lips have this way been."

When the seventh came to the bottom of his glass, and found there the ring, he looked at it, and knew that it was his father's and mother's, and said, "Oh that our little sister would but come! Then we should be free."

*"Who has eaten from my little plate?*
*And who has been drinking out of my little glass?"*

When the little girl heard this (for she stood behind the door all the time and listened), she ran forward, and in an instant all the ravens took their right form again; and all hugged and kissed each other, and went merrily home.

# THE YOUTH WHO FELT NO FEAR

A certain father had two sons: the elder was smart and sensible, and could do everything, but the younger was stupid and could neither learn nor understand anything; people said: "There's a fellow who will give his father some trouble!" When anything had to be done, it was always the elder who was forced to do it; but if his father bade him fetch anything when it was late, or in the nighttime, and the way led through the churchyard or any other dismal place, he answered: "Oh no, father, I'll not go there, it makes me shudder!" for he was afraid.

But when stories were told by the fire at night which made the flesh creep, and listeners would say: "Oh, it makes us shudder!" the younger sat in a corner and listened with the rest of them, and could not imagine what they meant. "They are always saying: 'It makes me shudder, it makes me shudder!' It does not make me shudder," thought he. "That, too, must be an art of which I understand nothing!"

Now it came to pass that his father said to him one day: "Hearken to me, you fellow in the corner there, you are growing tall and strong, and you too must learn something by which you can earn your bread. Look how your brother works, but you do not even earn your salt."

"Well, father," he replied, "I am quite willing to learn something—indeed, if it could be managed, I should like to learn how to shudder. I don't understand that at all yet."

The elder brother smiled when he heard that, and thought to himself: "Goodness, what a blockhead that brother of mine is! He will never be good for anything as long as he lives! He who wants to be a sickle must bend himself betimes."

The father sighed, and answered him: "You shall soon learn what it is to shudder, but you will not earn your bread by that."

Soon after this the sexton came to the house on a visit, and the father bewailed his trouble, and told him how his younger son was so backward in every respect that he knew nothing and learnt nothing. "Just think," said he, "when I asked him how he was going to earn his bread, he actually wanted to learn to shudder."

"If that be all," replied the sexton, "he can learn that with me. Send him to me, and I will soon polish him up."

The father was glad to do it, for he thought: "It will train the boy a little."

The sexton therefore took him into his house with the intention of having him ring the church bell. After a day or two, the sexton awoke him at midnight and bade him arise and go up into the church tower and ring the bell. "You shall soon learn what shuddering is," thought he, and secretly went there before him; and when the boy was at the top of the tower and turned round, and was just going to take hold of the bell rope, he saw a white figure standing on the stairs opposite the sounding hole.

"Who is there?" cried he, but the figure made no reply, and did not move or stir. "Give an answer," cried the boy, "or take yourself off; you have no business here at night."

The sexton, however, remained standing motionless so that the boy might think he was a ghost.

The boy cried a second time: "What do you want here? Speak if you are an honest fellow, or I will throw you down the steps!"

The sexton, not taking his threat seriously, uttered no sound and stood as if he were made of stone. Then the boy called to him for the third time, and as that was also to no purpose, he ran against him and pushed the ghost down the stairs, so that it fell down the ten steps and remained lying there in a corner. Thereupon he rang the bell, went home, and without saying a word went to bed and fell asleep.

The sexton's wife waited a long time for her husband, but he did not come back. At length she became uneasy, and wakened the boy, and asked: "Do you know where my husband is? He climbed up the tower before you did."

"No, I don't know," replied the boy, "but someone was standing by the sounding hole on the other side of the steps, and as he would neither give an answer nor go away, I took him for a scoundrel, and threw him downstairs. Just go there and you will see if it was he. I should be sorry if it were."

The woman ran away and found her husband, who was lying moaning in the corner, and had broken his leg.

She carried him down, and then with loud screams she hastened to the boy's father. "Your boy," cried she, "has been the cause of a great misfortune! He has thrown my husband down the steps so that he broke his leg. Take the good-for-nothing fellow out of our house."

The father was terrified, and ran thither and scolded the boy. "What wicked tricks are these?" said he. "The devil must have put them into your head."

"Father," he replied, "do listen to me. I am quite innocent. He was standing there by night like one intent on doing evil. I did not know who it was, and I entreated him three times either to speak or to go away."

"Ah," said the father, "I have nothing but unhappiness with you. Go out of my sight. I will see you no more."

"Yes, father, right willingly, wait only until it is day. Then will I go forth and learn how to shudder, and then I shall, at any rate, understand one art which will support me."

"Learn what you will," replied the father, "it is all the same to me. Here are fifty thalers for you. Take these and go into the wide world, and tell no one from whence you come, or who your father is, for I have reason to be ashamed of you."

"Yes, father, it shall be as you will. If you desire nothing more than that, I can easily keep it in mind."

When the day dawned, therefore, the boy put his fifty thalers into his pocket, and went forth on the great highway, and continually said to himself: "If I could but shudder! If I could but shudder!" Then a man approached who heard this conversation which the youth was holding with himself, and when they had walked a little farther to where they could see the gallows, the man said to him: "Look, there is the tree where seven men have married the ropemaker's daughter, and are now learning how to fly. Sit down beneath it, and wait till night comes, and you will soon learn how to shudder."

"If that is all that is wanted," answered the youth, "it is easily done; and if I learn how to shudder as fast as that, you shall have my fifty thalers. Just come back to me early in the morning." Then the youth went to the gallows, sat down beneath it, and waited till evening came. And as he was cold, he lighted himself a fire, but at midnight the wind blew so sharply that in spite of his fire, he could not get warm. And as the wind knocked the hanged men against each other, and they moved backwards and forwards, he thought to himself: "If you shiver below by the fire, how those up above must freeze and suffer!" And as he felt pity for them, he raised the ladder, and climbed up, unbound one of them after the other, and brought down all seven. Then he stoked the fire, blew it, and set them all round it to warm themselves. But they sat there and did not stir, and the fire caught their clothes. So he said: "Take care, or I will hang you up again." The dead men, however, did not hear, but were quite silent, and let their rags go on burning. At this he grew angry, and said: "If you will not take care, I cannot help you, I will not be burnt with you," and he hung them up again each in his turn. Then he sat down by his fire and fell asleep, and the next morning the man came to him and wanted to have the fifty thalers, and said: "Well, do you know how to shudder?"

"No," answered he, "how should I know? Those fellows up there did not open their mouths, and were so stupid that they let the few old rags which they had on their bodies get burnt."

Then the man saw that he would not get the fifty thalers that day, and went away saying: "Such a youth has never come my way before."

The youth likewise went his way, and once more began to mutter to himself: "Ah, if I could but shudder! Ah, if I could but shudder!"

A waggoner who was striding behind him heard this and asked: "Who are you?"

"I don't know," answered the youth.

Then the waggoner asked: "From whence do you come?"

"I know not."

"Who is your father?"

"That I may not tell you."

"What is it that you are always muttering between your teeth?"

"Ah," replied the youth, "I do so wish I could shudder, but no one can teach me how."

"Enough of your foolish chatter," said the waggoner. "Come with me, I will see about a place for you."

The youth went with the waggoner, and in the evening they arrived at an inn where they wished to pass the night. Then at the entrance of the parlor the youth again said quite loudly: "If I could but shudder! If I could but shudder!"

The host who heard this laughed and said: "If that is your desire, there ought to be a good opportunity for you here."

"Ah, be silent," said the hostess, "so many prying persons have already lost their lives, it would be a pity and a shame if such beautiful eyes as these should never see the daylight again."

But the youth said: "However difficult it may be, I will learn it. For this purpose indeed have I journeyed forth."

He let the host have no rest, until the latter told him that not far from thence stood a haunted castle where anyone could very easily learn what shuddering was if he would but watch in it for three nights. The king had promised that he who would venture to do so should have his daughter to wife, and she was the most beautiful maiden the sun shone on. Likewise in the castle lay great treasures, which were guarded by evil spirits, and these treasures would then be freed, and would make a poor man rich enough. Already many men had gone into the castle, but as yet none had come out again. Then the youth went next morning to the king, and said: "If it be allowed, I will willingly watch three nights in the haunted castle."

The king looked at him, and as the youth pleased him, he said: "You may ask for three things to take into the castle with you, but they must be things without life."

Then he answered: "Then I ask for a fire, a turning lathe, and a cutting board with the knife."

The king had these things carried into the castle for him during the day. When night was drawing near, the youth went up and made himself a bright fire in one of the rooms, placed the cutting board and knife beside it, and seated himself by the turning lathe. "Ah, if I could but shudder!" said he. "I fear I shall not learn it here either."

Towards midnight he was about to poke his fire when something cried suddenly from one corner: "Au, miaow! How cold we are!"

"You fools!" cried he, "what are you crying about? If you are cold, come and take a seat by the fire and warm yourselves."

And when he had said that, two great black cats came with one tremendous leap and sat down on each side of him, and looked savagely at him with their fiery eyes. After a short time, when they had warmed themselves, they said: "Comrade, shall we have a game of cards?"

"Why not?" he replied, "but just show me your paws." Then they stretched out their claws. "Oh," said he, "what long nails you have! Wait, I must first cut them for you." Thereupon he seized them by the throats, put them on the cutting board, and screwed their feet fast. "I have looked at your fingers," said he, "and my fancy for card-playing has gone," and he struck them dead and threw them out into the moat.

But when he had made away with these two, and was about to sit down again by his fire, out from every hole and corner came black cats and black dogs with red-hot chains, and more and more of them came until he could no longer move, and they yelled horribly, and got on his fire, pulled it to pieces, and tried to put it out. He watched them for a while quietly, but at last when they were going too far, he seized his cutting knife, and cried: "Away with you, vermin," and began to cut them down. Some of them ran away, the others he killed, and threw out into the moat. When he came back he fanned the embers of his fire again and warmed himself. And as he thus sat, his eyes would keep open no longer, and he felt a desire to sleep. Then he looked round and saw a great bed in the corner. "That is the very thing for me," said he, and got into it. When he was just going to shut his eyes, however, the bed began to move of its own accord, and went over the whole of the castle. "That's right," said he, "but go faster." Then the bed rolled on as if six horses were harnessed to it, up and down, over thresholds and stairs, but suddenly hop, hop, it turned upside down, and lay on him like a mountain. But he threw quilts and pillows up in the air, got out, and said: "Now anyone who likes, may drive," and lay down by his fire, and slept till it was day.

In the morning the king came, and when he saw him lying there on the ground, he thought the evil spirits had killed him and he was dead. Then said he: "After all it is a pity—for so handsome a man."

The youth heard it, got up, and said: "It has not come to that yet."

Then the king was astonished, but very glad, and asked how he had fared. "Very well indeed," answered he; "one night is past, the two others will pass likewise."

Then he went to the innkeeper, who opened his eyes very wide, and said: "I never expected to see you alive again! Have you learnt how to shudder yet?"

"No," said he, "it is all in vain. If someone would but tell me!"

The second night he again went up into the old castle, sat down by the fire, and once more began his old song: "If I could but shudder!" When midnight came, an uproar and noise of tumbling about was heard; at first it was low, but it grew louder and louder. Then it was quiet for a while, and at length, with a loud scream, half a man came down the chimney and fell before him.

"Hallo!" cried he, "another half belongs to this. This is not enough!" Then the uproar began again, there was a roaring and howling, and the other half fell down likewise. "Wait," said he, "I will just stoke up the fire a little for you." When he had done that and looked round again, the two pieces were joined together, and a hideous man was sitting in his place. "That is no part of our bargain," said the youth, "the bench is mine." The man wanted to push him away; the youth, however, would not allow that, but thrust him off with all his strength, and seated himself again in his own place. Then still more men fell down, one after the other; they brought nine dead men's legs and two skulls, and set them up and played at ninepins with them. The youth also wanted to play and said: "Listen you, can I join you?"

"Yes, if you have any money."

"Money enough," replied he, "but your balls are not quite round." Then he took the skulls and put them in the lathe and turned them till they were round. "There, now they will roll better!" said he. "Hurrah! Now we'll have fun!" He played with them and lost some of his money, but when it struck twelve, everything vanished from his sight. He lay down and quietly fell asleep.

Next morning the king came to inquire after him. "How has it fared with you this time?" asked he.

"I have been playing at ninepins," he answered, "and have lost a couple of farthings."

"Have you not shuddered then?"

"What?" said he, "I have had a wonderful time! If I did but know what it was to shudder!"

The third night he sat down again on his bench and said quite sadly: "If I could but shudder." When it grew late, six tall men came in and brought a coffin. Then he said: "Ha, ha, that is certainly my little cousin, who died only a few days ago," and he beckoned with his finger, and cried: "Come, little cousin, come." They placed the coffin on the ground, but he went to it and took the lid off, and a dead man lay therein. He felt his face, but it was cold as ice. "Wait," said he, "I will warm you a little," and went to the fire and warmed his hand and laid it on the dead man's face, but he remained cold. Then he took him out, and sat down by the fire and laid him on his breast and rubbed his arms that the blood might circulate again. As this also did no good, he thought to himself: "When two people lie in bed together, they warm each other," so he carried him to the bed, covered him over and

*Then the youth seized the axe, split the anvil with one blow,*
*and in it caught the old man's beard.*

lay down by him. After a short time the dead man became warm too, and began to move. Then said the youth, "See, little cousin, have I not warmed you?"

The dead man, however, got up and cried: "Now will I strangle you."

"What!" said he, "is that the way you thank me? You shall at once go into your coffin again," and he took him up, threw him into it, and shut the lid. Then came the six men and carried him away again. "I cannot manage to shudder," said he. "I shall never learn it here as long as I live."

Then a man entered who was taller than all the others, and looked terrible. He was old, however, and had a long white beard. "You wretch," cried he, "you shall soon learn what it is to shudder, for you shall die."

"Not so fast," replied the youth. "If I am to die, I shall have to have a say in it."

"I will soon seize you," said the fiend.

"Softly, softly, do not talk so big. I am as strong as you are, and perhaps even stronger."

"We shall see," said the old man. "If you are stronger, I will let you go—come, we will try." Then he led him by dark passages to a smith's forge, took an axe, and with one blow struck an anvil into the ground.

"I can do better than that," said the youth, and went to the other anvil. The old man placed himself near and wanted to look on, and his white beard hung down. Then the youth seized the axe, split the anvil with one blow, and in it caught the old man's beard. "Now I have you," said the youth. "Now it is your turn to die." Then he seized an iron bar and beat the old man till he moaned and entreated him to stop, promising to give him great riches. The youth drew out the axe and let him go.

The old man led him back into the castle, and in a cellar showed him three chests full of gold. "Of these," said he, "one part is for the poor, the other for the king, the third yours."

In the meantime it struck twelve, and the spirit disappeared, so that the youth stood in darkness. "I shall still be able to find my way out," said he, and felt about, found the way into the room, and slept there by his fire.

Next morning the king came and said: "Now you must have learnt what shuddering is?"

"No," he answered; "what can it be? My dead cousin was here, and a bearded man came and showed me a great deal of money down below, but no one told me what it was to shudder."

"Then," said the king, "you have saved the castle, and shall marry my daughter."

"That is all very well," said he, "but still I do not know what it is to shudder!"

Then the gold was brought up and the wedding celebrated; but howsoever much the young king loved his wife, and however happy he was, he still said always: "If I could but shudder—if I could but shudder." And this at last angered her.

Her waiting maid said: "I will find a cure for him; he shall soon learn what it is to shudder." She went out to the stream which flowed through the garden, and had a whole bucketful of gudgeons brought to her. At night when the young king was sleeping, his wife drew the clothes off him and emptied the bucket full of cold water with the gudgeons in it over him, so that the little fishes sprawled about him. Then he woke up and cried: "Oh, what makes me shudder so? What makes me shudder so, dear wife? Ah! now I know what it is to shudder!"

# IRON HANS

There was once upon a time a king who had a great forest near his palace, full of all kinds of wild animals. One day he sent out a huntsman to shoot him a roe, but he did not come back. "Perhaps some accident has befallen him," said the king, and the next day he sent out two more huntsmen who were to search for him, but they too stayed away. Then on the third day, he sent for all his huntsmen, and said: "Scour the whole forest through, and do not give up until you have found all three." But of these also, none came home again, none were seen again.

From that time forth, no one would any longer venture into the forest, and it lay there in deep stillness and solitude, and nothing was seen of it, except sometimes by an eagle or a hawk flying over it. This lasted for many years, until an unknown huntsman announced himself to the king as seeking a situation, and offered to go into the dangerous forest.

The king, however, would not give his consent, and said: "It is not safe in there; I fear it would fare with you no better than with the others, and you would never come out again."

The huntsman replied: "Lord, I will venture it at my own risk, of fear I know nothing."

The huntsman therefore betook himself with his dog to the forest. It was not long before the dog fell in with some game on the way, and wanted to pursue it; but hardly had the dog run two steps when it stood before a deep pool, could go no farther, and a naked arm stretched itself out of the water, seized it, and drew it under. When the huntsman saw that, he went back and fetched three men to come with buckets to bale out the water. When they got to the bottom they saw lying there a wild man whose body was brown like rusty iron, and whose hair hung over his face down to his knees. They bound him with cords, and led him away to the castle. There was great astonishment over the wild man; the king, however, had him put in an iron cage in his courtyard, and forbade the door to be opened on pain of death, and the queen herself was to take the key into her keeping. And from this time forth everyone could again go into the forest with safety.

The king had a son of eight years, who was once playing in the courtyard, and while he was playing, his golden ball fell into the cage. The boy ran thither and said: "Give me my ball."

"Not till you have unlocked the door for me," answered the man.

"No," said the boy, "I will not do that; the king has forbidden it," and ran away.

The next day he again went and asked for his ball; the wild man said: "Open my door," but the boy would not.

On the third day the king had ridden out hunting, and the boy went once more and said: "I cannot open the door even if I wished, for I have not the key."

Then the wild man said: "It lies under your mother's pillow, you can find it there."

The boy, who wanted to have his ball back, cast all thought to the winds, and brought the key. The door opened with difficulty, and the boy pinched his fingers. When it was open the wild man stepped out, gave him the golden ball, and hurried away.

The boy had become afraid; he called and cried after him: "Oh, wild man, do not go away, or I shall be beaten!"

The wild man turned back, took him up, set him on his shoulder, and went with hasty steps into the forest.

When the king came home, he observed the empty cage, and

asked the queen how that had happened. She knew nothing about it, and sought the key, but it was gone. She called the boy, but no one answered. The king sent out people to seek for him in the fields, but they did not find him. Then he could easily guess what had happened, and much grief reigned in the royal court.

When the wild man had once more reached the dark forest, he took the boy down from his shoulder, and said to him: "You will never see your father and mother again, but I will keep you with me, for you have set me free and I have compassion for you. If you do all I bid you, you shall fare well. Of treasure and gold have I enough, and more than anyone in the world."

He made a bed of moss for the boy on which he slept, and the next morning the man took him to a well, and said: "Behold, the gold well is as bright and clear as crystal; you shall sit beside it, and take care that nothing falls into it, or it will be polluted. I will come every evening to see if you have obeyed my order."

The boy placed himself by the brink of the well, and often saw a golden fish or a golden snake show itself therein, and took care that nothing fell in. As he was thus sitting, his finger hurt him so violently that he involuntarily put it in the water. He drew it quickly out again, but saw that it was quite gilded, and whatsoever pains he took to wash the gold off again, all was to no purpose. In the evening Iron Hans came back, looked at the boy, and said: "What has happened to the well?"

"Nothing, nothing," he answered, and held his finger behind his back, that the man might not see it.

But he said: "You have dipped your finger into the water; this time it may pass, but take care you do not again let anything go in."

By daybreak the boy was already sitting by the well and watching it. His finger hurt him again, and as he stooped his head over it, unhappily a hair fell down into the well. He took it quickly out, but it was already quite gilded. Iron Hans came, and already knew what had happened.

"You have let a hair fall into the well," said he. "I will allow you to watch by it once more, but if this happens for the third time then the well is polluted and you can no longer remain with me."

On the third day, the boy sat by the well, and did not stir his finger, however much it hurt him. But the time was long to him, and he looked at the reflection of his face on the surface of the water. And as he bent down more and more, trying to look straight into the eyes, his long hair fell down from his shoulders into the water. He raised himself up quickly, but the whole of the hair of his head was already golden and shone like the sun. You can imagine how terrified the poor boy was! He took his pocket-handkerchief and tied it round his head, in order that the man might not see it.

When he came back he already knew everything, and said: "Take the handkerchief off." Then the golden hair streamed forth, and let the boy excuse himself as he might, it was of no use. "You have not stood the trial and can stay here no longer. Go forth into the world, there you will learn what poverty is. But as you have not a bad heart, and as I mean well by you, there is one thing I will grant you; if you fall into any difficulty, come to the forest and cry: 'Iron Hans,' and then I will come and help you. My power is great, greater than you think, and I have gold and silver in abundance."

Then the king's son left the forest, and walked by beaten and unbeaten paths ever onwards until at length he reached a great city. There he looked for work, but could find none, and he learnt nothing by which he could help himself. At length he went to the palace, and asked if they would take him in. The people about court did not at all know what use they could make of him, but they liked him, and told him to stay. At length the cook took him into his service, and said he might carry wood and water, and rake the cinders together.

Once, when it so happened that no one else was at hand, the cook ordered him to carry the food to the royal table, but as he did not like to let his golden hair be seen, he kept his little cap on. Such a thing as that had never yet come under the king's notice, and he said: "When you come to the royal table you must take your hat off."

He answered: "Ah, lord, I cannot; I have a bad sore place on my head."

Then the king had the cook called before him and scolded him, and asked how he could take such a boy as that into his service; and that he was to send him away at once. The cook, however, had pity on him, and exchanged him for the gardener's boy.

And now the boy had to plant and water the garden, hoe and dig and bear the wind and bad weather. Once in summer when he was working alone in the garden, the day was so warm he took his little cap off that the air might cool him. As the sun shone on his hair it glittered and flashed so that the rays fell into the bedroom of the king's daughter, and up she sprang to see what that could be.

Then she saw the boy, and cried to him: "Boy, bring me a wreath of flowers."

He put his cap on with all haste, and gathered wild field flowers and bound them together.

When he was ascending the stairs with them, the gardener met him, and said: "How can you take the king's daughter a garland of such common flowers? Go quickly, and get another, and seek out the prettiest and rarest."

"Oh, no," replied the boy, "the wild ones have more scent, and will please her better."

When he got into the room, the king's daughter said: "Take your cap off, it is not seemly to keep it on in my presence."

He again said: "I may not, I have a sore head."

She, however, caught at his cap and pulled it off, and then his golden hair rolled down on his shoulders, and it was splendid to behold. He wanted to run out, but she held him by the arm, and gave him a handful of ducats.

With these he departed, but he cared nothing for the gold pieces.

He took them to the gardener, and said: "I present them to your children, they can play with them."

The following day the king's daughter again called to him that he was to bring her a wreath of field flowers, and when he went in with it, she instantly snatched at his cap, and wanted to take it away from him, but he held it fast with both hands. She again gave him a handful of ducats, but he would not keep them, and gave them to the gardener for playthings for his children. On the third day things went just the same; she could not get his cap away from him, and he would not have her money.

Not long afterwards, the country was overrun by war. The king gathered together his people, and did not know whether or not he could offer any opposition to the enemy, who was superior in strength and had a mighty army.

Then said the gardener's boy: "I am grown up, and will go to the wars also, only give me a horse."

The others laughed, and said: "Seek one for yourself when we are gone—we will leave one behind us in the stable for you." When they had gone forth, he went into the stable, and led the horse out; it was lame of one foot, and limped hobblety jib, hobblety jib; nevertheless he mounted it, and rode away to the dark forest.

When he came to the outskirts, he called, "Iron Hans" three times, so loudly that it echoed through the trees. Thereupon the wild man appeared immediately, and said: "What do you desire?"

"I want a strong steed, for I am going to the wars."

"That you shall have, and still more than you ask for."

Then the wild man went back into the forest, and it was not long before a stable-boy came out of it, who led a horse that snorted with its nostrils, and could hardly be restrained, and behind there followed a great troop of warriors entirely equipped in iron, and their swords flashed in the sun. The youth handed over his three-legged horse to the stable-boy, mounted the other, and rode at the head of the soldiers. When he got near the battlefield a great part of the king's men had already fallen, and little was wanting to make the rest give way. Then the youth galloped thither with his iron soldiers, broke like a hurricane over the enemy, and beat down all who opposed him. They began to flee, but the youth pursued, and never stopped, until there was not a single man left. Instead of returning to the king, however, he conducted his troop by byways back to the forest, and called forth Iron Hans.

"What do you desire?" asked the wild man.

"Take back your horse and your troop, and give me my three-legged horse again." All that he asked was done, and soon he was riding on his three-legged horse.

When the king returned to his palace, his daughter went to meet him, and wished him joy of his victory. "I am not the one who carried away the victory," said he, "but a strange knight who came to my assistance with his soldiers." The daughter wanted to hear who the strange knight was, but the king did not know, and said: "He followed the enemy, and I did not see him again."

She inquired of the gardener where his boy was, but he smiled, and said: "He has just come home on his three-legged horse, and the others have been mocking him, and crying: 'Here comes our hobblety jib back again!' They asked, too: 'Under what hedge have you been lying sleeping all the time?' and he replied: 'I did the best of all, and it would have gone badly without me.' And then he was still more ridiculed."

The king said to his daughter: "I will proclaim a great feast that shall last for three days, and you shall throw a golden apple. Perhaps the unknown man will show himself."

When the feast was announced, the youth went out to the forest, and called Iron Hans.

"What do you desire?" asked he.

"That I may catch the king's daughter's golden apple."

"It is as safe as if you had it already," said Iron Hans. "You shall likewise have a suit of red armor for the occasion, and ride on a spirited chestnut horse."

When the day came, the youth galloped to the spot, took his place among the knights, and was recognized by no one. The king's daughter came forward, and threw a golden apple to the knights, but none was able to catch it but he, only as soon as he had it he galloped away.

On the second day, Iron Hans equipped him as a white knight, and gave him a white horse. Again he was the only one who caught the apple, and he did not linger an instant, but galloped off with it. The king grew angry, and said: "That is not allowed; he must appear before me and tell his name." He gave the order that if the knight who caught the apple should go away again, they should pursue him, and if he would not come back willingly, they were to cut him down and stab him.

On the third day, he received from Iron Hans a suit of black armor and a black horse, and again he caught the apple. But when he was riding off with it, the king's attendants pursued him, and one of them got so near him that he wounded the youth's leg with the point of his sword. The youth nevertheless escaped from them, but his horse leapt so violently that the helmet fell from the youth's head, and they could see that he had golden hair. They rode back and announced this to the king.

The following day the king's daughter asked the gardener about his boy. "He is at work in the garden; the queer creature has been at the festival too, and only came home yesterday evening; he has likewise shown my children three golden apples which he has won."

The king had him summoned into his presence, and he came and again had his little cap on his head. But the king's daughter went up to him and took it off, and then his golden hair fell down over his shoulders, and he was so handsome that all were amazed.

"Are you the knight who came every day to the festival, always in different colors, and who caught the three golden apples?" asked the king.

"Yes," answered he, "and here the apples are," and he took them out of his pocket, and returned them to the king. "If you desire further proof, you may see the wound which your people gave me when they followed me. And I am likewise the knight who helped you to your victory over your enemies."

"If you can perform such deeds as that, you are no gardener's boy; tell me, who is your father?"

"My father is a mighty king, and gold have I in plenty as great as I require."

"I well see," said the king, "that I owe my thanks to you; can I do anything to please you?"

"Yes," answered he, "that indeed you can. Give me your daughter to wife."

The maiden laughed, and said: "He does not stand much on

ceremony, but I had already seen by his golden hair that he was no gardener's boy," and then she went and kissed him.

His father and mother came to the wedding, and were in great delight, for they had given up all hope of ever seeing their dear son again.

And as they were sitting at the marriage feast, the music suddenly stopped, the doors opened, and a stately king came in with a great retinue. He went up to the youth, embraced him, and said: "I am Iron Hans, and was by enchantment a wild man, but you have set me free: all the treasures which I possess, shall be your property!"

# THE ELVES AND THE SHOEMAKER

There was once a shoemaker, who worked very hard and was very honest, but still he could not earn enough to live upon; and at last all he had in the world was gone, save just leather enough to make one pair of shoes.

Then he cut his leather out, all ready to make up the next day, meaning to rise early in the morning to his work. His conscience was clear and his heart light amidst all his troubles; so he went peaceably to bed, left all his cares to heaven, and soon fell asleep. In the morning after he had said his prayers, he sat himself down to his work, but to his great wonder, there stood the shoes, all ready made, upon the table. The good man knew not what to say or think at such an odd thing happening. He looked at the workmanship; there was not one false stitch in the whole job; all was so neat and true, that it was quite a masterpiece.

The same day a customer came in, and the shoes suited him so well that he willingly paid a price higher than usual for them; and the poor shoemaker, with the money, bought leather enough to make two pairs more. In the evening he cut out the work, and went to bed early, that he might get up and begin betimes next day; but he was saved all the trouble, for when he got up in the morning the work was done ready to his hand. Soon in came buyers, who paid him handsomely for his goods, so that he bought leather enough for four pair more. He cut out the work again overnight and found it done in the morning, as before; and so it went on for some time: what was got ready in the evening was always done by daybreak; and the good man soon became thriving and well off again.

One evening, about Christmastime, as he and his wife were sitting over the fire chatting together, he said to her, "I should like to sit up and watch tonight, that we may see who it is that comes and does my work for me." The wife liked the thought; so they left a light burning, and hid themselves in a corner of the room, behind a curtain that was hung up there, and watched what would happen.

As soon as it was midnight, there came in two little naked dwarfs; and they sat themselves upon the shoemaker's bench, took up all the work that was cut out, and began to ply with their little fingers, stitching and rapping and tapping away at such a rate, that the shoemaker was all wonder, and could not take his eyes off them. And on they went, till the job was quite done, and the shoes stood ready for use upon the table. This was long before daybreak; and then they bustled away as quick as lightning.

The next day the wife said to the shoemaker: "These little wights have made us rich, and we ought to be thankful to them, and do them a good turn if we can. I am quite sorry to see them run about as they do; and indeed it is not very decent, for they have nothing upon their backs to keep off the cold. I'll tell you what: I will make each of them a shirt, and a coat and waistcoat, and a pair of pantaloons into the bargain; and do you make each of them a little pair of shoes."

The thought pleased the good cobbler very much; and one evening, when all the things were ready, they laid them on the table, instead of the work that they used to cut out, and then went and hid themselves, to watch what the little elves would do.

About midnight in they came, dancing and skipping, hopped round the room, and then went to sit down to their work as usual; but when they saw the clothes lying for them, they laughed and chuckled, and seemed mightily delighted.

Then they dressed themselves in the twinkling of an eye, and danced and capered and sprang about, as merry as could be; till at last they danced out at the door, and away over the green.

The good couple saw them no more; but everything went well with them from that time forward, as long as they lived.